This is the story of a most unusual relationship; Fala the Slider Girl and Bartek her Watcher. No mere chance has brought them together, it is their destiny. Although neither knows it, theirs is a love as deep as the oceans and as enduring as Gaia, our earth which birthed and protects them. But the time is coming when Gaia will be threatened by a far greater power. To resist, Gaia will need their courage, and she will demand they both sacrifice their all, including each other.

This book is a work of fiction. Names, characters, places, and incidents either are products of the author's imagination or are used fictitiously. Any resemblance to actual events or locales or persons, living or dead, is entirely coincidental.

Slider Girl
Copyright © 2019 Jack Crux
ISBN: 978-1-4874-2390-2
Cover art by Martine Jardin

Published by eXtasy Books Inc or
Devine Destinies, an imprint of eXtasy Books Inc

Look for us online at:
www.eXtasybooks.com or www.devinedestinies.com

Slider Girl
Weird Fishy Tales Book 1

By

Jack Crux

DEDICATION

For Mother and Father

PROLOGUE

In the beginning, it did not matter.

Nothing that had happened was important, not until she came into being.

She was one of many, but she was different. She was special and the universe would burn because of it.

Cherished, precious, beloved beyond words, she was the flicker that lit a million suns, the fire creating the energy that fuelled the universe. And such power overwhelmed her entirely. Insolent and confident within the heat of her presence, she could blow life into the weakest ember or scorch it into oblivion with the fury of a dying star. She laid waste to her world, giving great powers of destruction to her people but torturing them endlessly should they falter and fail in her schemes. They worshipped her with all the dread and horror that true divinity can bring and presented their very souls to her, gave her everything, even their capacity for individual thought, until they became a hive with only one consciousness—hers. They died willingly, brutally climbing over the twisted, burnt-out corpses of their brethren to do her bidding.

It was not enough for her.

It was never enough.

Soon, bored and disinterested, finding no satisfaction with the wonders she had been given, she sent her spark outwards like the insignificant cosmic dust that drifted on the solar winds, to conquer the rest of the universe. To subjugate and enslave her sisters, the ones like her but not like her, be they great or small, who had not been given such a magnificent gift as hers.

Borne on flames of violence and hate, unmoved by even the most tragic of circumstances, her fire devoured all that stood in its path,

1

leaving behind worlds enslaved and barren, razed to ash and cinders, fit only for the habitation of her own mindless minions.

The doctrine was always the same. Her people arrived in peace as sophisticated benefactors. They meant no harm, bringing gifts of civilisation, of progress, which they were willing to share. Whether embraced with awe and wonder or suspicion and defiance, the ending was monotonously predictable—the indigenous culture would be forgotten, overwritten and obliterated, the natives beholden, enslaved, unable to live without her fire.

Then it was a simple matter of taking what she required, which was everything, always.

Many worlds, many civilisations, be they just on the first step of development or already evolved into a complex, compelling society, were her targets. And the sister whose people she took, whose planets she enslaved, no matter how hard they tried to resist, would eventually succumb to the inevitable and be consumed into the all-encompassing flame, their powers enriching her own.

That was her favourite part, to emphasise her domination, her superiority, for there was no one like her.

Not really.

And she would triumph over all.

Her inferno raged across the universe. Nothing could stop it.

So many worlds, so much terror. She was completely insensitive to any of it. Unyielding and obstinate in her desire to conquer all but excruciatingly dissatisfied when she did, her tedium and imperviousness to the suffering she created would be her downfall because, on a small, insignificant, green and blue planet, where her follower had been delivering her dogma for centuries, something astonishing was about to happen . . .

CHAPTER ONE

It wasn't his face that piqued her attention, although with its striking cheekbones, proud mouth, and strong nose, it was achingly beautiful. Neither was it his inky-black hair, unfashionably short. Not his slim angular body caught at the end of the long years of transition from boy to man, nor his perfectly shaped buttocks that begged to have a hand squeeze them. He was more than bonny, it was true.

All these things retained her interest but did not ensnare her gaze, did not capture her attention as surely as a hook through the lip of a fish.

No.

It was his eyes . . .

There was nothing quite so depressing as an English seaside town, once the drunken day-trippers and fighting families had scuttled back to the cities for their winter. Fala mused as, answering the overpowering pull deep in her soul, she wandered through the insipid grey for most of the morning. As she walked, the wearying weight of her loss threatened to smother her like a rolling sea fog. Her dull, aching chasm of grief made it easy to ignore the tatty amusements desperately flashing their gaudy lights and playing infuriatingly catchy tunes at her through the murky mist, the frighteningly forlorn laughing policeman machine, cackling loud enough to penetrate the peace of any child's dreams, was one nightmare too many.

And yet Fala sensed more mundane fears roaming the de-

3

serted streets, so that the sense of desperation was palpable, the shopkeepers and businessmen losing all hope for a summer, now long gone, that had never delivered where it mattered, in their accounts. The town was tottering on the very edge of despair. All who could have, had already left the dirty streets for something better, and only the truly hopeless remained, flotsam washed ashore with no means of re-floating itself.

Fala fit right in.

Periodically, as if to add to her despondency, the salty rain blown in from the sea threatened to engulf everything in large, smattering spots. Earlier, for a time the sun had managed to fight through the dense cloud to bring a shadowy ethereal light to proceedings and lift Fala's mood but towards noon even it had given up as if the energy needed to keep the sepia gloom at bay was too much and it retreated, swallowed by the cloud as the dreary rain set in.

Fala was miserable and cold, far deeper than the marrow of her bones. The temperature did not touch her, never had. She did not fail to be invigorated by a swim in even the coldest ocean. It was the paucity of spirit that sapped her strength, threatened her purpose. Danger could be anywhere. Her enemies were ruthless and efficient, and they thrived on the thrill of the hunt. Failure and intense loneliness stalked her as she shunned all human contact and simply stood staring out from the pier, a solitary figure almost indistinguishable in the grey, lost to the pull of the ocean and the memories that haunted her.

Eventually, sodden and shivering, she allowed her feet to take her where they would, and she shuffled into the last cafe at the end of the pier. To her surprise, it smelt of warmth and safety in a way few places did, but such unexpected comfort caused the warning bell inside her to clang harshly.

Something was amiss.

Something was about to happen.

Accepting fate with the stoicism of one who had previously tried and failed to change it, she chose a table by the window, shook off her saturated jacket like a dog emerging from the water and sat down.

She ignored her internal alarm's continuing dull peal with a studied indifference that silenced both her dread and her expectation. The need for accompaniment and love were both directly at odds with the weary acceptance of what such a relationship would bring.

She had been alone for too long and she was as tired as death. She lacked the will to begin again.

And then she saw those eyes.

Every colour of the ocean swirled there, from the sparse chilly silver grey of the poles shrouded in ice and fog at the very edges of the world to the brilliant blue balmy warmth of the tropics.

Alluring and so dangerous.

Fala tried to look away, she really did, to reject the hope that rushed through her as those beautiful orbs held her glance challengingly, but she was already lost. Lost in their depth, their current and their colour, flowing, swirling, pulling her in like the most hazardous whirlpool in the deepest water.

They were stealing her breath, reaching into her chest and snatching hold of her heart, claiming it with the sheer unfounded audacity of a thief in the night. Even now, taking her old and broken spirit and infusing it with life, with youth and vigour, the promise was enough to send a flutter through her, borne on butterfly wings of expectation.

It was already too late.

Those intense eyes called to her with both the fire of passionate partnering and the piercing loneliness of one forlorn gull riding the wind high in the sky. The salty tang of her past, never far from her mind, gripped her, plummeting her down into an abyss of sorrow for all she had lost, warring with the mesmerising promise of a future—the clutching longing to feel the heat of togetherness and companionship once more.

She drew back, counselled herself with her father's words as old as the wind, *What is conceived with love, dies in pain and fear.*

She had spent lifetimes proving the simple wisdom learnt in her childhood. However hot the initial fire, the scorching desire, however violently the flames danced, eventually they would lose their energy and fade and die. Only the cold, bleak ashes of sorrow and loss would remain.

Ashes of sorrow and loss.

And yet that was all she had.

He sauntered towards her, and it was a definite saunter, as if he were here only by necessity and there were many other places he would prefer to be. But she saw in his loquacious stride, and the hint of swagger, the man he would become, her rock, her protector, her saviour, if she would allow it.

She closed her eyes, banishing the scene, and him to nothing, as if in doing so she could halt the course she had set by coming to this town, satiating her need to feel the sea, choosing this particular café, as if she could free him from the burden of destiny that already claimed him.

She wanted to run, to leave him to his ignorance, to an insignificant life with no fear and no glory, but she knew she would not.

The universe gave her what she needed, exactly when she needed it, and today it had given her—him.

"What can I get you?" His voice was of a higher pitch than she had imagined, wavering between the carefree child he had been and the worry-worn guardian he would become.

She felt chillingly old and ashamed. What right did she have to steal him away from his life and family? To take away his youthful ambitions and dreams? To tie him so tightly to her that he would know no grace save in her own comfort, and feel no contentment except when she allowed it? But she looked up into those eyes and lost herself once more in the echoes of the past she found there, her heart constricting painfully in her chest as the shaft of sweet loss pierced her anew. He looked so much like her lost ones, and that memory brought only the withering cold of failure and utter defeat, a cold dagger thrust into the bottom of the spine, bringing instant paralysis.

Pushing the bitter pain away to the dark shadows at the edges of her mind, she cleared her throat.

"Fish, please," she said.

His face quirked into a puzzled expression, the eyebrows above those remarkable eyes lifting in a formidable question that he would never ask. Already, although he did not understand what was happening, the changes in him were beginning. Like any mortal, instinctively he fought them. "And chips?" he managed to ask, seeking sanctuary in the mundane as if it could win over the power of destiny.

She smiled and noted how his mouth curled up in response and his body relaxed a little. "No thank you, and no batter. Just naked fish, please."

"Naked." He gulped. The act of swallowing appeared to have become very hard for him and yet still, he fought it. "Mushy peas? Something to drink?"

She shook her head, recognising his dogged determination to serve. She let the command voice coat her words just a little. "Go get it, please."

He stiffened, nodded curtly and turned away. She

watched him weave between the tables, hips swaying sleek-ly, a man at the very beginning of his life's mission, although he did not know it.

She allowed herself the luxury of a selfish smile. She hadn't been wrong about that ass.

He returned minutes later, a shaking hand placing the stark white fish, almost the same colour as the plate it lay on, in front of her. "Thank you," she said. "What's your name?"

"Bart Buchan?" he replied with an intonation at the end turning his response into a question. Already he sought her approval, even for his name.

It could not be.

Her world fluttered like a rupture in time, the scene shimmering before her eyes as the thrill rushed through her. This was unexpected. "Short for Bartosz?" she asked, work-ing hard to keep her voice calm as the memories thundered through her.

He shrugged. "Nah, just Bart. My mother liked the Simpsons."

She chuckled. The universe had a horrifically sick sense of humour and didn't she know it. He smiled, ridiculously pleased that he had made her happy although unsure how and her heart cried out for him. This poor, lost soul. How little he knew, doomed forever to serve her in an impossible quest.

"You not from round here, then?" he asked, words clipped as if he had difficulty getting them out.

"No," she replied.

"Thought so . . ." He hesitated like an old man suddenly losing his balance and afraid to take a forward step. She waited, as a palette of deep emotions coloured his features, knowing that her presence had been the catalyst for great changes in his very being as his long-dormant DNA sought to fulfil its potential. He was changing, though none could

8

see it except her. She wanted to leave. She wanted to walk away, to release him from a contract he did not know had been made but now the change had been set in motion. In doing so, she would condemn him to an even greater torment. He would wander the world forever, searching until he found her again. So she waited as his hand went to his head. His body shivered and he bit back a gasp.

A family of five bustled in from the sodden elements and sat down by the window amidst a flurry of half-inflated water wings and buckets and spades that dripped murky puddles on the cheap lino flooring. They were all whingeing.

"I want ice cream."

"No, it's too cold."

The youngest child began to cry, his mother making soothing clucking noises to placate him. The middle kid knocked over the plastic menu card, which slapped to the ground and caused a corresponding rumble of anger to erupt from the frazzled father, while the older one didn't even bother to look up through his greasy fringe as he killed another dozen aliens on his battered Game Boy.

Fala ignored them, her attention fully focused on Bart who lurched to the table, reaching out to steady himself, his eyes flashing wide with confusion and fear. She held his gaze once more, her eyes calming and confident, soothing him. She felt the ties knotting together, weaving into a tapestry of mutual support, binding them together for the rest of his life.

A memory emerged from the jumbled chaos of the past in her mind and with melancholy, she recalled such a joining in other times—the ceremony, the pure and unsullied joy of her people at such a momentous event, the feasting, the hope, and happiness. But that was all lost, claimed by the swirling mists of time and defeat. She was the only one left to remember that sweet celebration.

Now, she thought bitterly, the event happened unnoticed, unseen in the greasy chip shop at the end of the pier, the ocean the only remaining constant as it lapped below like a thirsty tiger, perhaps just a little less grey than it had been previously.

"Bart!"

She knew he didn't hear, too lost in the depths of her gaze. The noise of the sea swirling in his ears, he swayed slightly as if he stood on the prow of one of those beautiful big sailing ships that used to fly across the water, borne on the very breath of the wind in times gone by.

"Bart!" The voice was gruff and came from behind the glass cabinet that held a selection of deep-fried jewels—golden battered fish, fish cakes sparkling in vinegar and ingot-shaped sausages, all to be paired off with a trove of chips to make a true culinary treasure.

"Customers!"

She released him then and he gulped, Adam's apple bobbing in his pale throat below his face, still set in grim confusion.

"Go. Do what you have to do," she commanded softly.

"But . . ."

"I will wait."

Still he hesitated, licking his lips nervously. "Who are you?" he asked.

She smiled, recalling the end of the ceremony, the words he spoke, the part he played, although he did not know it. "I am Fala."

"Fala," he repeated, rolling the word around his tongue, getting used to it as if it was a new pair of boots. "Who am I?" he asked.

By magic, the whole firmament seemed to suddenly shift as though it had released an unexpectedly deep sigh. Silence fell over the chip shop as hearts stopped for a second and a blanket of well-being fell over the whole building. Everything paused for a glorious moment, the universe took a well-deserved rest.

At that moment, a glass, untouched, tumbled to the floor from the family's table and shattered noisily. And with that, the enchantment seemed to lift. The muted chat returned slightly cheerier than before, and the family, baffled, inspected the remains of the broken glass on the tiles before them.

Fala knew the significance of the moment, the power that was in a name. In the old days, it would have all been foreordained and planned before the joining ceremony, a name of portent and of meaning, of significance to the couple. She floundered as wanting fought with need in her mind. She could not call him Bartosz. That name was forever bathed in wanting and wreathed in the bitter pain of defeat for her. She would doom no other with its history but this one was so like him. His aura shone more brightly than any watcher she had known since.

And she should honour his mother whose seemingly innocent love of a yellow American cartoon boy had been a step on the path that had unknowingly led her son to this place.

Finally, she gave in to the need which pulled at her all the way from a long-forsaken grave atop a barren Scottish hill, many, many years away.

"You are my Bartek."

CHAPTER TWO

Ten years later . . .

The thumping pain was growing, from the middle of her hot forehead and radiating through every sinew, bringing with it the familiar wave of nausea that slowed her steps and caused her vision to waver nightmarishly.

The itch solidified to a deeper desire—the call of the water, the need to break out, and immerse herself in the coolness, feel it flow over her feverish skin, calm her, massage her, make her whole once more.

The need—oh, the need.

Fala ignored all of the familiar symptoms, pushing herself onward along the busy pavement heaving with shoppers piled high with Christmas presents and good cheer.

The smell of roasting horse chestnuts sweetened an atmosphere made ugly by greedy commercialism and incessantly overplayed Christmas tunes, insidiously flowing out to the street from every shop.

It was her own fault.

She had been a fool, but the lure of pretty things had always been her weakness. And she had known the shops were so very close, just a quick uphill walk and a turn to the left and the departmental stores of untold pleasures awaited her.

How could a girl refuse?

An hour before, unable to rest, she had fidgeted around the hotel room. Looking out through its long Edwardian windows at the people below, who with collars up and heads down, shuffled by in the gathering gloom of the winter's day, so far north it could be dark just after three at this time of year. A tram stopped outside, its bell ringing a mournful warning in the damp air.

Nobody paid any heed.

Nobody ever did.

She sighed, restless beyond words, unable to quell the feelings of gathering deep dread and the pull of being this close to the ocean. She had ignored both of them for too long, and now the price must be paid.

She had turned back to the room. It was modern and well-appointed, stark greys and whites, colourful art prints on the wall, sleek wooden flooring, covered under the bed by a deep rug—

Scarlet. The colour of blood.

The colour of her dreams.

There was no comfort to be found in it.

A door to her left led to the bathroom where she knew a frigid, white, porcelain bath waited for her. It was no luxury for her but a prerequisite wherever she stayed. A shower was no good.

The thought caused the familiar itch deep within. She ignored it with practised skill and instead decided on a far riskier but just as enjoyable action.

Bartek had been sleeping, snoring softly, spread out on the bed, uncharacteristically vulnerable and uncontrolled, his hand twitching absently as the latent energy sought to escape his mortal frame. He was exhausted from the overnight drive through trying, sleety conditions.

She had hesitated before leaving, to drink in the craggy angles and shadows of his face, his long eyelashes, so often eclipsed by the limitless beauty of his eyes taking her full attention as they lushly guarded his closed lids, and the straight line of his mouth, bordered by dark stubble, set hard, grimacing slightly even in the haven of sleep.

She let the memory of his smile warm her chilly heart.

Once he had laughed a lot, been a child of summer, bright, shining with a sunny warmth and almost every sentence finished with a self-deprecating chuckle. Eager to learn and impress her, he had learnt his lessons well, fulfilling every expectation she had of him.

He had become what she required and in doing so, all too soon, winter had set in as the grim realities of her struggle had stolen both the frivolous joy from him and the vicarious happiness it had given her.

He didn't laugh like he used to, and rarely even smiled. She missed the boy he had been, with all the regret that swelled her culpable heart. And she silently mourned his loss.

He would be angry at her giving into temptation, at her even contemplating running such a risk, submitting to her base desires, being weak where he demanded she be strong, but that did not stop her. The fury of his wrath would soon blow itself out, she knew—a violent but short-lived storm. It had never stopped her from doing what she wanted and it never would.

If there was no time to appreciate the beauty of this world, the wonders of creation, everything else, all the struggle, was rendered pointless. They might as well give up and let their enemies win.

So, planting a brief chaste kiss on his cheek, she left the hotel room as he groaned softly in his sleep but did not waken.

Ignoring the salty cold wind that blew the scent of the Forth, so achingly close, to tempt her, she turned instead towards the teeming business of Princes Street a few days before Christmas.

For as long as she could remember, she had needed to connect intimately with nature. It was the wonder of life she loved, the memory of her father and the gifts he had bestowed on an ungrateful populace. Not the man-made synthetics but the genuine leather, the silk and the fur, even the wool. She stood in the scarfs section of the first, glaringly lit, department store she had come across, smiling sadly as she ran her pale hands over the materials. A thousand stories danced within the fibres below her fingertips and she knew them all, the sacrifice and the pain that had been woven together, captured, enslaved and silenced to become mere items of clothing.

Like a child in a candy store, she gasped in delight as she moved through the shop to the jewellery section, finding a display wholly devoted to coral. She vaguely remembered a shimmering workshop, but the memory floated away and the colours took her attention. So many colours, so many shapes and so many stories. She wished she could touch and communicate with the little creatures, at least feel the echo of their presence but the signage was very clear and besides she knew they were long gone. Only the beautiful husks of their labour remained.

Saddened, she moved on to regard the pearls.

Fala was so lost in her emotions that she almost missed the tell-tale signature of a meddler, far too close for comfort. But reliable and strong as ever, her alarm cut through her reverie to bring her back to the danger of the present.

She glanced around, apparently unconcerned, but every sense vibrating with the inexplicable yet intoxicating thrill of possible competition.

The meddler watched her from near the stairs. Fala recognised her from previous pursuits, Kristianne, a slip of a girl with dead eyes blackened by kohl and addiction, skin flaky, already decaying on her pathetic frame, a shadow of a life, as pale as the grave, and messy blue hair piled on her head.

For a second their eyes met and Fala saw the girl flinch in shock when she sensed the pure power of her quarry, realised she would not be taken by her spell alone. Taking advantage of the weakness, Fala threw a mystic fog at the girl, then turned and left the shop as quickly as she could without attracting attention, for where there was a meddler there would surely be bruisers, too.

Back out on the street, Fala moved towards the hotel and sure enough sensed the signature of bruisers, five or six at least, all moving towards where she stood.

She cursed her own weakness and flashed a psychic warning to Bartek. Then she moved into the crowd, hoping to lose herself in the general melee and untapped seething emotion of the people around her.

It was then she felt her strength leaving her. Her legs grew heavy and it was all she could do to move with the crowd. Glancing over her shoulder, she glimpsed the meddler behind her, and following her gaze, picked out a weaver, hiding in the doorway of a shop further down the street.

His eyes were unblinking points of intense light in the darkness of the hood masking the rest of his face. They focused on her, stony with concentration as he spun the spell to entrap her.

Something was wrong.

Ten weavers would not be enough to hold her, and yet this one's spell was so strong, it sucked the energy from her limbs, replacing it with an overwhelming need for water with his weave.

Panic, absolute and brittle, rushed through her. A man carrying a large package he could not see over slammed into her and almost sent her flying. She clasped hold of the waste bin that loomed in front of her to right herself, all the time calling out to Bartek, praying he would come.

Finding it increasingly difficult to concentrate, her heart thundering, she stumbled across the road, tripping slightly over the tram tracks. Above her, the craggy battlements of the old castle were menacing shadows in the darkening sky. They looked on, unflinching, indifferent. They had seen too many dramas, too many tragedies to be moved by any now.

She made her way towards the stalls, made of polished pine, of the Christmas market, bright lights and the aromas of frying onions and mulled wine beckoning her on. The Salvation Army band played *O Come All Ye Faithful*, eclipsed for a moment by the discordant hoot from a train on the tracks below.

A homeless soul, wrapped in plastic and a dirty tartan blanket, thrust out his hand, brittle, twig-like fingers clutching at her coat as she passed, but she hurried on as fast as her weakening strength would allow.

It was getting harder to move, harder to think as the dismal fog of the weave descended upon her like a shroud over a corpse. Despite herself, she admitted this weaver was good, but she was too debilitated to examine his signature further.

She needed all of her strength to stay ahead of her hunters.

It had begun to snow. Small white pellets of ice, sparkling diamonds falling on the chill northerly breeze, could be picked out between the yellow of the street lights.

Like a watercolour left out in the rain, Fala's world appeared smudged, imperfect, as if everything had been pared back to the basic elements. White light and deep dark, stark and colourless, panic and survival, life and death, all threatened to overcome her resistance as she fought to maintain her control.

Through the stalls to her left, she caught sight of a bruiser, big and ugly, making his way toward her. She checked her direction and turned towards the Scott Memorial, fighting to stop the vomit from swirling up into her gullet and gulping it back. Fear threatened to take her as it grew more difficult to move her legs.

Another bruiser approached from Princes Street, so near she could sense the excitement steaming off him in reeking waves, feeling the awful blackness that claimed him.

She turned again, determined to make her way down to the gardens as her mind whirled, trying to make sense of what was happening, of how she had been trapped so easily. Why hadn't she sensed their presence sooner? What had masked their psychic signatures?

Unbidden, the defeatist thought she had no wish to acknowledge swirled in her mind anyway. Resolutely she pushed it away.

This could not be the end. Surely, after all she had been through, after all the years, the defiant fight, it could not end here.

She stopped, jeans splitting, her legs suddenly moulded together, unable to move further. It was difficult to stand, so she leaned against another black iron waste bin, cold against her feverish scaly, skin.

She fired off a warning, a burst of energy that shocked the bruisers. She sensed them retreat, surprised by her attack.

But it did not stop them for long.

Already they were surging forward, three from her left, two at her right and one in front of her. The meddler, too, an evil grin of triumph revealing her blackened teeth, lurked behind them, eager to claim a part in any success. There was no sign of the weaver but judging by the strength of his spell, he must still be near.

Fala drew in a deep breath.

Everything felt too hard.

She had no energy to keep her form or consciousness, let alone her fight. A weariness so devastating it stole her purpose, seeped into the marrow of her bones. The bruisers were only feet away. Time seemed to slow as she felt the paralysing fear of the fox before the hounds, knew the moment of supreme vulnerability before their teeth ripped her to bloody pieces.

It was all lost.

Suddenly mayhem, loud and violent, thrust its way into her surrendering psyche. The disciplined playing of the band halfway through *O Little Town of Bethlehem* descended into chaos as members dived out of the way.

Women screamed and men shouted angrily and then another noise reached her eardrums—the deep guttural roar of a trail bike.

It seemed to materialise in front of her. Strong arms grabbed her and pulled her close. With an overwhelming sense of relief, she recognised the signature, the scent of strength and safety, unusually overlaid this time with the stench of burning oil and the pop of the idling engine, but she lacked the energy to move toward him. Undaunted, Bartek bent forward to scoop her up and lay her rigid body across the petrol tank in front of him.

"Hold on," he commanded, pulling her arms around his neck. With the renewed vigour that his presence had brought, she did so.

He gunned the motor and the bike shot forward, mowing down the nearest bruiser as he reached out to grab them. Bartek's well-placed boot knocked over another as they flew by. Then they were clear and he threw the bike through the panicked crowd, narrowly missing diving bodies until they were out onto the road.

Ignoring the *no entry* sign, he pivoted on his left leg, broadsided to the right, swerved past the oncoming, indignantly hooting buses and cars and then up a steep alleyway, over cobbles and steps, to catapult out on to the Royal Mile, narrowly missing a startled couple apparently sharing the same putrid burnt orange outfit, he the trousers and she the coat, both with identical citrus stripy scarves.

Bartek accelerated away amidst aghast tourists and locals alike as Fala closed her own eyes, ignoring the water pull inside her, diverting every last shred of her strength to cling onto him as they bumped up the street towards the castle.

He rode the bike with great skill and sheer bravado as if he had stolen it, which of course, he had, ignoring all the vehicles and the frenzied pedestrians, not to mention the traffic signs, until he sensed her relax and knew the spell was broken, the weaver left well behind.

Only then did he turn to follow the road that looped around the castle, through the lingering hoppy fumes of the nearby brewery and back down to the new town.

Discarding the bike in an alleyway, he lifted her still boneless body with the greatest care and carried her to the hotel and straight up to the bathroom. Fala rested her head on his shoulder, her body feeling shattered into tiny, unconnected shards of glass.

He lay her down into the bath with infinite gentleness as if on to a bed of the softest rose petals and turned on the tap. Precious water, lukewarm, gushed over her limp, twitching body, bringing with it the salvation she craved. She sighed weakly, closed her eyes and held on to his strong hand.

The room filled with the smell of the ocean, brine, and barnacles as she relaxed and reverted to her natural form, her scaly tail where her legs had been, shimmering in the bright light with all the rainbow allure of the most valuable jewels.

Finally, she let the exhaustion take her and she gave herself up as she had so many times before to Bartek's tender loving care.

CHAPTER THREE

She lay back into the water, letting the unbidden memories float her away from the moment. Memory was the sanctuary of a coward. Her childhood studies had taught her that, but she could not agree.

There was nothing that lacked courage in her memory. She knew why it came to her now, why her psyche sought to retreat from the future as the grinding wheel of time continued its unstoppable circular movement. Thirteen years was the cycle that brought her back. The present and the past were the same and so would be the future.

She had lived these days before and she shivered because she sensed the doom they would bring.

She opened her eyes, looked at her Bartek kneeling on the cold tiles beside the bath, pale in the bathroom's dim light, with concern only for her. She noted the deep lines around his eyes and at the corners of his mouth, lines that had once cracked into an enchanting smile, now deepened with worry. He was always so attentive and yet she longed for what he had lost, the boy he had been.

The years fell away and she recalled those first days after they had met. He had accepted her invitation to escape the soggy seaside town, forsaken his college course, and left the smelly room in the equally smelly house without the slightest hesitation.

They had gone south, searching for warmer waters. Her body relished the moment they stepped off the plane into the relative heat of the Canaries, the tart tang of the sea, borne on the soft breeze, calling to her, always calling to her.

"I can't swim," he had disclosed the first night at the hotel's terrace bar as her body prickled with wonderful heat and she desperately controlled the urge to rush down to the beach and dive into the rolling surf.

"Really?" She had laughed at the little mockeries the universe liked to throw up.

He sipped his beer, a sweet blush of embarrassment colouring his cheeks. She wasn't even sure if he was actually old enough to legally drink it but he had asked for it in his deepest voice and the barman had served it so she hadn't questioned him any further.

He gulped and continued, "My mother wouldn't let me go. She wrote notes to the school so I didn't have to."

"Why ever not?"

He shrugged, disarming and boyish, and she felt her heart tighten a further notch at his sweet innocence. "She said my family had an aversion to water. My uncle drowned and my grandfather's brother, too."

Fala nodded slowly. She had heard it before. The women of many seafaring families reacted in exactly the same way when their menfolk were taken. She supposed it was natural. Silently she wondered how his mother would cope now that her son had fulfilled the same destiny as his unfortunate male forebears. Would she say he had drowned, too? In a way he had.

"What about your father?" she asked.

"Never knew him. He was a sailor, just passing through."

"Was he?" She rolled her eyes. The repercussions of that needed to be investigated further but not now. Now, she could no longer resist the pull to the sea. "So, I guess he was okay with water."

Bartek chuckled. "I guess so."

"Come on," she continued. "I'll teach you."

"What now? In the middle of the night? It's dark."

"Yes, I have something to show you. A secret, something important . . ."

Of course, he could swim, he just didn't know it and he was brave enough to trust her, even in those early days. He followed her into the darkness, the exhilarating roll of the breakers and the pull of the current drawing him in, knocking him from his feet. He grasped hold of her hand, went under a few times and came back up spluttering and coughing and soon they were past the breaking of the waves out into the calm undulation of the deeper ocean.

"Let the water take you," she murmured into his ear.

He complied, floating and kicking his legs. He let out a whoop of sheer joy.

"I can do this," he shouted wildly at the magnificent ocean, so vast and unfathomable before him. He was all youthful exuberance and boyish delight, the energy pulsing off his aura like the beam from a lighthouse on a stormy night.

He did make her young again, like the ones who had gone before, and Fala joined in his laughter.

"You can. You were born for this!" And then she winked at him, threw her tail in the air and dived downwards into the water.

Bartek, hair plastered down on his head and water dripping from his nose, was still gaping when she came back up a few moments later. "My god," he spluttered. "You've got a weird fishy tail!"

She reached out and took hold of his shoulders, drawing him into her. "You have much to learn," she whispered in his ear, knowing he would hear her silky voice even over the roar of the breakers. "But I will teach you."

He would always hear her voice, even when they were apart.

Indeed, over the years that followed, he had always heard and answered her call, saved her many times from her enemy, the Shape Shifter and his ever-enclosing net. With a shudder, Fala came back from the memory of the warm evening in the pounding surf, when anything had seemed possible, back to the empty, silent bathroom, aware that he was no longer with her.

She was utterly alone.

The water around her had turned from a soothing balm to a barely tepid bath. She sighed. A stranger, alone in both her worlds, she pulled her tail in, slid back into her legs once more and used her arms to push herself out of the tub.

Bartek was sitting on the bed, eating a burger and fries he must have ordered from room service, when she pulled the dressing gown about herself and left the moist sanctuary of the bathroom. A wave of nausea rushed through her at the smell of the meat but she quickly quelled it. Sometimes he did such things. She was sure it was his way of rebelling, of flexing his masculinity and exerting his individuality in one of the only avenues she had left open to him.

She wouldn't deny him his moment.

"You took a risk coming back here," she said mildly.

He shrugged, depositing a chip in his mouth defiantly. "Hide in plain sight," he muttered. Neither spoke what both knew—she had been in too bad a state for him to risk taking her any further. The bath water had been an absolute must.

She sighed, moved towards him and placed a fleeting kiss on his forehead. "I taught you well. Thank you."

He stood up, moved to the kettle, clicked it on. "All part of the service. Although why the hell shopping is so important I will never understand." He still retained the humour he had possessed when she had first met him but it had matured from the unrestrained fizz of a bubbly wine to the ironic bite of an aged, dour whisky. "Looks like we made the news," he nodded toward the TV bolted to the wall in the corner, now switched off. "Apparently it was a drunken prank. Damn students."

She rolled her eyes at him and sat in the seat he indicated. He placed a platter of pink whole prawns in front of her and retreated back to the bed, the kettle now boiling with its throaty song and the rumble of a tram outside the only noises in the increasingly morbid silence of the room.

Pushing away her disquiet by focusing on her condition, Fala realised just how hungry she was. Still she ate the prawns slowly, picking them apart with intricate care as if dwelling on them could somehow blank out the worry that her previous escapade had engendered. Bartek finished his meal and made her a hot chocolate after the kettle boiled, his loud, violent stirring of the liquid the tell-tale sign that he was as concerned with events as she was.

Finally, he sat back on the bed and eyed her expectantly. "We need to leave."

"Yes." She sipped the chocolate.

Oh, delicious sugar—a poison that could kill her but another temptation she found hard to resist and one that Bartek had taken it upon himself to ration accordingly. He read her so well, knew at this moment as fear and desperation bit hard, the long-term risk to her system could be justified by the instant shot of saccharine comfort.

He waited, motionless, patient in her silence. He had long ago stopped asking questions, content that she would tell him what he needed to know, when he needed to know it.

She felt a wave of guilt that she withheld so much from him and yet, she was secretive by nature. It came with her past, embedded in her DNA. Too much treachery through the years had painfully taught her the power of information. What he did not know he could not betray, as others had before him, should the worst things happen. Still, he deserved her trust. He had earned it time and time again. And yet, though she refused to acknowledge it, the ever-present doubt, planted in her long ago by the abandonment to her greatest enemy of the one closest to her, still lay dormant, biding its time in the very depths of her mind.

"We continue north," she said.

He bit his lip, looked away. "He knows your destination."

"Assuredly."

She lifted her fork and played with the remains of the prawns. Chasing black dead eyes around her plate seemed somehow appropriate. She moved her other hand to stroke her stomach. "Time is running out."

She saw it then in Bartek's eyes, just a flicker, just for a moment until he restrained it. Disappointment had etched the blue with bitterness and again a wave of regret washed through her.

"The weaver was strong," he said, choosing, as ever, to ignore his own feelings as irrelevant and instead focus on the practical. She nodded in answer to both his question and his reaction. How she cherished him for his devotion, his control, his lack of self-pity.

"Too strong. It was almost as if—" She stopped, put down her fork.

Bartek waited. Silence never phased him. He never felt the need to fill it. He was as patient as the grave, living his life in the pregnancy of a pause, forever trapped in the moment before the intimate touch, the hot, aching longing before the ecstasy of fulfilment.

She shook her head. "No. It couldn't be."

She shuddered, the mere thought that the Shape Shifter could be so close sent spikes of frozen fear down her spine. And yet why wouldn't he be? He would be drawn to her as time ran out, like all the other times.

She stood up, the chair scraping loudly on the slick

wooden floor. "We need to go and go now," she ordered.

"I'm ready," he replied, with no hint of exasperation that she had instructed him.

With a deep sigh, she moved towards him and ran her hands down his back, drinking him in, taking his energy to enliven her battered soul. He shuddered at her touch but succumbed willingly.

Finally, when she had taken enough, he stepped away, disconnecting with a slight stumble. He covered it by nodding towards the new pair of jeans he had laid out on the dressing table stool for her. She sighed in resignation. Ruining her pants was a frequent occupational hazard for a mermaid and they had both come to accept and plan for it long ago.

CHAPTER FOUR

Fala found the drive north from Edinburgh as monotonous as the dark that surrounded them. There was nothing to see, nothing to focus on, the road stretching out in an almost straight line squeezed between the ominous black fields pressing in on either side.

Occasionally the emptiness was lit by the orange of street lights streaking by but they highlighted nothing of interest. Fala felt as if the outside world had ceased to exist. All that remained was the smelly warmth of the cab in which they sat.

Loretta—although Fala suspected her real name was more likely to be Kirsty-Marie judging by her broad Glaswegian accent—the wee tartan trucker with whom they had hitched the lift, was a friendly sort but when her enquiries were met with monosyllabic answers that gave no fuel to any possible juicy gossip, she got the point, stopped talking about the fact that social media was full of stories of a mermaid in Princes Street and gave up, reverting to playing her much loved country music CDs at such a level that the whole cab seemed to vibrate in time with the bass guitar.

Seemingly forgetting both her passengers, she sang all of the tear-jerking stories in a fake American accent and at an eye-watering pitch that belied the size of her petite Scottish lungs, often stopping in mid-song to swear profusely at a road user who apparently needed input from her superior driving skill.

Slouched behind her, with one massive paw draped regally over her shoulder, was a big, cuddly, messily salivating dog that she introduced as Gatlin who intermittently howled along to the music.

Fala sat in the middle. She still felt wrung out and deflated, used up in every possible way. The feeling of deja vu haunted her. She had travelled this road before and followed where it led, to stand on the impressive rocks and walk in the clinging clumps of dune grass as sharp as a knife at their destination. She had suffered her great defeats there and yet still she returned, to suffer again.

She glanced at Bartek but he was hunched away from her, watching the chill raindrops run down the window as if they were the most interesting things he had ever seen. She nestled into his warmth and he adjusted his position to accommodate her but did not turn. Clearly, he did not want to speak, so she closed her eyes and let the flight of memory take her where it would.

She found herself back in a small French village which hugged the coast of the Mediterranean Sea. The addictive giggle of school kids from the playground behind drifted in with the morning sun to the small apartment where she sat. They had rented the beautiful space above one of the small cafes right on the seafront. From the top of the white stone walls, beautiful purple flowers cascaded downwards and unselfishly shared their luxurious scents with the passers-by. Fala had lingered too long, she knew, but the closeness to the waves, the ancient cobbled streets that all led down to the sea, and the peacefulness that such a place engendered had captivated her. She wanted so much to stay that she had allowed that desire to influence her better judgement.

As was his routine Bartek had popped down to the patisserie on the corner for fresh breakfast croissants and she sat on the little balcony surrounded by pots and flowers, eyes closed as the sun anointed her with its perfect touch. *Why couldn't it always be like this?*

The peace was shattered on one particular day by the front door being smashed open. She looked up to see two figures silhouetted against the azure sky beyond. Fear sent icy fingers into her heart and she stood up with a gasp as she realised the front figure was Bartek.

He was taut, body tight as a bowstring, on the very edge of panic, his head pulled back to expose his vulnerable throat. She saw the tell-tale glimmer of the blade there. She watched, mesmerised, as the silver metal pressed into his pale skin, stretching it until a single ball of red blood bubbled to the surface to balance motionless on the steely edge of the knife.

"What do you want?" she demanded, focusing her attention on to the mysterious figure that held the boy.

It was completely obscured by the billowing black cloak it wore. Dark and foreboding, it seemed to be drawing in the light, absorbing it, turning it to something rancid and rotten. Fala recognised the stench instantly and understood why she had not sensed the presence sooner. It was a cloaked murmurer—a messenger only but still a sign that they had been found. Her enemies knew where she lingered.

She drew on her courage, prepared herself, and waited. Regardless, his voice, when it came, even across the miles to be amplified through the empty vessel of the murmurer before her, caused the hairs on the nape of her neck to stand up and a cold shudder to rush through her.

"You've found a new *gadger*, Fala." It was a mild accusation of displeasure, a fatherly criticism that dripped disappointment. "Will you never learn?"

"Let him be," Fala responded.

She could sense the fear in Bartek, saw him shivering, his eyes flashing wild and wide, and his hands flexing impotently at his sides as the murmurer held him immobile.

"It's you that should let him be," the voice rumbled. "But

you just can't help yourself, can you? Remember how it always ends, Fala? Don't you get tired of repeating the same mistakes again and again?"

She was fascinated by the bubble of blood on Bartek's neck. She stared as it grew until it formed a teardrop-shaped drip that hovered, caught in time for a moment and then suddenly slipped to meander down towards the top of his t-shirt. It picked up speed as he gulped violently, trying to adjust his position to fight back, but the murmurer gripped him tightly.

"Do you taste his delicious fear, Fala?"

She could detect the sound, like a licking of lips.

"He's a feisty one, this one," the voice continued. "Different from the others. A strange aura. Maybe you should consider where he comes from."

Fala hesitated, hating herself for being tempted, but asked the question anyway. "What do you mean?"

"You are always too quick to trust, my dear Fala. You need to learn restraint."

"And you are always too quick to mock. Let him go."

"Very well." The murmurer pulled back the knife and for one horrific moment, Fala thought it would slit the beautiful, bulging throat that lay before it but instead it pushed Bartek forward into her arms. She caught him, heard the sigh of relief the boy tried so desperately to bite back as she felt the dread, rich and robust, still thrumming through his veins.

"Take the boy if you must, Fala, but do not trust him, for you know every gadger will fail, will let you down. In the end, there is only one being worthy of you."

The figure before them suddenly puffed outwards, the black cloak that concealed all of its features ballooning as if caught by a stray breeze and then, with a magical flurry, it disappeared entirely, leaving only the shiny sharp knife marooned in a puddle of slimy black wax congealing on the floor.

"Damn!" Bartek breathed with feeling as he stared disbelievingly at the beguiling blade. A trace of his own blood glistened on the waxy substance for a second, like petrol on a rain puddle, before it was absorbed into the darkness as the whole mess solidified and then decomposed into a small pile of grey ash.

"We have to go, now." Fala gently pushed him forward as she moved but Bartek remained still. "*Now!*"

"No," he said softly but firmly, rooted to the spot like an immovable oak, his mouth curled in petulant schoolboy revolt, shaking his head. "Not until you explain it all to me."

She glanced over her shoulder, as if to support her argument by pointing out that more danger threatened to enter, but the hallway was empty. The door hung at an awkward angle on broken hinges, swaying slowly to the resonant song of a nearby wind chime.

"I will, but not here."

He eyed her, his hand going up to his throat to dab at the stream of blood, obviously debating with himself whether he should press the point. Inevitably duty won. "All right," he answered finally. "We can make the afternoon train. But you will tell me everything on the way?"

She nodded.

Everything was such an all-consuming word. It ate up all flexibility and revealed all the places she needed to hide. She would tell him only what was necessary to know.

He held her gaze and flexed his fingers. "I will never feel that defenceless ever again," he vowed solemnly.

CHAPTER FIVE

Sometimes Fala hated the transient life she was forced to live.

Never able to stay in one place, unable to lay down any roots, her material belongings were sparse, just a few clothes neatly folded and painstakingly packed into an old cloth bag that she had carried around with her for centuries.

Bartek had left behind everything he owned to follow her and it took only seconds for him to stuff his few t-shirts and extra pair of jeans into his shabby rucksack. He seemed to sense the urgency in Fala and they were soon abandoning the homely little flat.

"What about payment? The landlord?" He tried to lift the door back on to its broken hinges and failed.

"Leave it," Fala responded.

"But—"

"All will be well."

They caught the rattler that had changed little from the previous times Fala had travelled this way. She mused to herself it was seemingly a ghost train trapped in a moment in time, doomed to endure while all else changed around it. It laboriously followed the meandering rail tracks westwards, stopping at each village along the beautiful coast. The guard hurriedly smoked a foul-smelling Gaulloise at every stop, the lung-choking smoke drifting lazily on the light breeze through the carriages, before using what little breath he had left to blow his whistle to restart the rattling of the train. Each time, he dissolved into fits of coughing, hacking up dark flecks of phlegm and blood onto his once paper white handkerchief as he awkwardly climbed aboard.

With no air conditioning and apparently precious little suspension, the journey wasn't the most comfortable but Bartek didn't seem to mind. After shoving their bags on to the overhead luggage rack, he sat opposite her, his longer fingers impatiently drumming on the table.

She smiled at his annoyance, at his need to know. How many times had she begun a conversation similar to this one? *Once every thirteen years* was the precise answer. Each conversation had gone differently, depending on the listener, but rarely had she spoken to an audience so rapt as this one.

Now, tortured by old wounds, she remembered the cloaked murmurer's words. *This one is different.* What did it mean? What was different about Bartek, apart from his absolutely alluring youthful energy?

She hesitated, probed his aura again but could sense nothing in him that should not be there. No bleakness or treachery, only a colourful ambiguity. She had to assume he was the real thing.

"I'm going to go back to the beginning," she said.

He nodded. "I like history," he disclosed. "All Kings and battles and stuff."

She rolled her eyes. "This won't be quite like the history you learnt at school. When you live it, it tends to be a great deal messier, so I will keep to the facts, mostly."

"What's a *gadger*?" he asked.

"Are you always this impatient?" she responded.

The disarming shrug again. Bartek pressed on resolutely. "The . . . thing with the knife, that was what he called me, wasn't it?"

Fala looked out the window, blinded for an instant by the purity of the sun shimmering on a glassy sea. She bit back the natural urge that hummed through every sinew of her body to go to it, took a deep breath of the stuffy, smoky air in the carriage and brought her gaze back to Bartek.

"It's a disrespectful term that my enemies use." She reached out, took hold of both of his hands across the table, squeezed them gently. "I prefer *watcher*."

"Watcher? I'm a watcher?"

She simply nodded.

"What do I watch?"

She held his unblinking stare. "Me."

He screwed up his face in confusion. "You?"

"Maybe if you'd let me start at the beginning, where I meant to, it would be a little clearer."

She squeezed tighter, feeling his hands, sweaty and clutching at her, like his mind grabbing for the truth. "You have to learn to trust me, Bartek. I have done this before."

He flinched away far too violently for such a gentle rebuke and she was mindful of how difficult it was for him. He was predisposed to serve her at a very base level, but that message, as yet, had not been accepted by the higher parts of his brain.

He was like a frisky young colt, all flaring nostrils, and wild eyes, who needed breaking to the saddle, but there was an art to that. Too little discipline and he would remain wild and unreliable, but too much and he would be afraid and damaged beyond repair—useless to her either way.

"I'm sorry," he said, looking away, gulping. "It's just . . ."

"I understand," she soothed and reaching up, stroked his cheek. "It will get easier, I promise."

"Will it? Really?" There was no place to hide from the beautiful clarity of his gaze.

She nodded at his insight. "In some ways, yes. In others, not so much."

"Why me?"

His mind was jumping around, seeking answers to questions that were not yet fully formed, seeking a peg of knowledge on which to hang his heavy coat of curiosity.

She smiled despite herself, as he pressed on. "Why did you choose me?"

"I didn't."

"You didn't? Then who?"

"Your history chose you, the culmination of all the things that brought you to the place where you met me." She fixed him with her most serious stare. "The universe chose you." As she said the words, something felt wrong, out of place, but she quashed it and turned her concentration back to him.

He sat back, a look of disbelief clouding his face. "Wow."

"Now, do you want to learn the truth or are you going to keep interrupting me?"

The disbelief faded from his face, chased away by a self-conscious smile and the hint of embarrassment. He looked down shyly. His hand freed itself from hers and went to cover his mouth, and he shuffled nervously, uncomfortable on the stained and faded train seat.

God, Fala thought, he was quite beautiful.

She felt the unbidden smile crack her stern mask once more. It was so difficult to be serious with him, his youthful exuberance mesmerising in every way.

As if sensing her attraction to him, he matched her smile. "So, tell me the history that I didn't learn at school."

And she did, as the train continued to rattle westwards and the guard interrupted them to check their tickets, and to point out to them in stuttering English when they passed the village graveyard where, when the time came, and it surely was not far away, as he choked and spluttered, he would be buried alongside all of his ancestors who had died over the last three centuries.

The sheer beauty of their surroundings, even the sweaty

heat and discomfort of the journey, and the interrupting guard were lost in the fantastical web she wove.

It was a story she had refined with practise to wide brush strokes that took in great wedges of time in single sentences. She gave only the facts, pared back the emotion, the hurt and the pain, that were irrevocably entwined with her past.

She told him of a world before humans came out of the swamps, when her people, called the fisherfolk, frolicked in every ocean, and the air was filled with hope, a time when anything was possible.

She spoke of the serious work they had done in filling the seas with marine life, and then of the days when the boring burden of endless time ticking away resolutely burned away her people's vigour, changed hope to bitterness, turned them from creators of wonder to destroyers. It had choked their purity of purpose as her people fell under the yoke of accumulating power, of stealing energy from the rest of the planet, and only a few remained true to their original aims.

And she told of the alien, the visitor from the stars, the Shape Shifter, G'llaha, who crash-landed on their world.

Initially welcomed and treated as a friend, he reinvigorated the fisherfolk. He gave them shortcuts, ways to find new energy, taught them how to shift their shape, to replace their tails with legs and their gills with lungs, but ultimately, he betrayed them in the most brutal of ways, stealing from them the very essence of their being—their power.

He enslaved them and killed them and raised up a new species from the swamps—humans, whom he could manipulate and thus take over the world.

Bartek listened intently, accepting what she said as truth in the way that his genes were programmed to do. "An alien from the stars?" he said finally. "Wow, so the truth really is out there."

She raised her eyes quizzically.

"*X Files*," he said. "Another of my mother's favourite shows. I guess I'm lucky she didn't call me Fox."

Fala shook her head. "She watched a lot of TV?"

"Never switched it off. Died in front of it. Had a heart attack when her favourite character got killed off unexpectedly. Missed the end to her favourite show. I guess that would have pissed her off, big time, especially as it was a fake death. The character came back in the last season to get the girl but my mother . . . she remained quite dead."

Bartek shook his head and took a long swig from the water bottle. His callous flippancy could not hide the obvious pain behind his words. He sniffed and moved on and Fala realised that was his method of coping. "Can he really shapeshift?"

"Oh yes. And many other things besides."

"Was he the one that spoke to you today?"

"Yes, through a cloaked murmurer. He has a whole network of beings, some human, some less so. Weavers who weave spells, bruisers who are really hired muscle, I guess, and meddlers, who . . . well, meddle."

"Why is he after you?"

As she rocked back into the seat, a cloud of dust puffed lazily out of the faded upholstery like an old carpet half-heartedly hit with a brush. It hung in the air, snatching irritatingly at her nostrils, pricking tears at the edge of her eyes and suddenly she felt very old and tired.

A wave of despondency washed through her.

She drew in a deep breath, taking a small amount of power from Bartek's overwhelming aura, just to give herself the energy to continue.

Her voice was rooted in deep sadness and she could not hold his gaze but looked away to the sea when she finally answered.

"Because I have something he needs. He needs my power.

He has the rest." She gulped. "I am the only one left. I hold the secret. I am the last mermaid."

CHAPTER SIX

Fala had travelled this way many times and she had come to see that Aberdeen was a city seen at its best either on a bright sunny day or on a clear dark night, when the light of a chromium moon shone down from a soft velvet sky. Then the hard granite of the buildings engrained with sparkling mica dazzled in competition with the stars above, creating an air of magic not visible on a dull day when the mood of melancholy lingered like the depressing haar mist that rolled in from the sea.

It was a place that she had grown to love as it clung tenaciously to the land on the edge of the sea, hemmed in to the north and south by long sandy beaches and ragged, gaping cliffs. Its people were initially dour and suspicious, less welcoming than those from further south. Nevertheless they had a grim dignity and formable resilience not found elsewhere. They were hard to please but once committed, a loyal and supportive bunch.

Over the preceding thirty years there had been a significant change perceived by all, not just someone with the emotional astuteness, honed from many lifetimes of suffering, of the last mermaid. New money from oil had created a buoyant economy where the taxis were Mercedes, the cost of living was second only to London in the UK, strange accents had become commonplace and the usual Scot's caution about money had been somewhat overtaken by an overindulgence in profligacy.

Everyone, it seemed, had benefitted from the boom time

and when Fala had visited the last time she had seen them frittering their gains away as if they would last forever. But world economics had burst the bubble, the easier oil fields in the North Sea had been exhausted, the price of Brent Crude had plummeted and along with it — Aberdeen's wealth.

It pained Fala to know there were homeless scraps of humanity on Union Street and queuing at the Job Centres, and Loretta had explained as they entered the city limits, driving past the massive, empty granite mansions, *For Sale* signs hanging limply in overgrown gardens, that the oil millionaires had left the city's West End for richer pickings elsewhere.

Although for a time seduced by wealth and power, Fala suspected that Aberdeen had never truly forgotten its roots. She knew the city owed its existence to the sea and in its harbour, the waters of which lapped up almost to the main street, where once fishing boats had bobbed, great oil supply ships snoozed idly to the soporific gentle rise and fall of the tide, waiting for work, and the Orkney ferry chuffed black smoke into the dark sky while swallowing its nightly mixture of passengers bound for the islands.

It was to the docks that Loretta was headed and she stopped at the traffic lights to disembark her passengers. With a quick wave and a farewell smattered with obscenities, she was off to join the ferry line, leaving lung-clenching diesel fumes, the voice of Kenny Rogers and the howling of Gatlin to slowly dissipate in her wake.

The pungent tang of fish was always on the air and it re-exerted its dominance as the diesel residue faded. Fala pulled her coat around her and quelled a shiver and the urge, so strong, to plunge into the water nearby—a compulsion she had learned to tame over the years but would never lose.

Memories of this place, dire and depressing, fought to

gain a footing in Fala's mind but she swept them away with practiced ease. She told herself it was cold but nowhere near as cold as she had experienced in the past. The shudder was simply the product of the contrast between the sweaty warmth of the cab and the crisp cut of the northern wind that stole her breath.

Bartek, head hidden beneath his beanie, picked up both their bags from where he had dumped them in order to help her down from the cab and began to trudge up towards the brighter lights of Union Street.

She regarded his hunched back thoughtfully, wondering when he had become the leader and she the follower. Somewhere in the ten long years they had travelled together, she had given up the responsibility, letting him shoulder it along with all of the other cares. There was nothing new in that. It was part of his role, part of the reason he watched. Those before him had done it just as uncomplainingly as he and yet it annoyed her that she could not pinpoint the time, the day, when she had allowed him to take the lead.

She knew why her mind was acting in such a way, and why it was re-living their time together. That, too, was part of the cycle. It was the prologue to losing him. She shuddered again, stricken by the sudden fear. Could she survive such a devastating blow?

He stopped, and, realising she was not beside him, he turned, eyes reflecting the yellow glow of the street light, instantly concerned. "I'm sorry . . ." he began.

She sniffed, shook her head, banishing the demon of her doubts. She had lost many before him and she would lose many after. He was expendable. She, on the other hand, was not. That was simply the truth of it and neither of them could change it. It always felt this bad as the cycle drew to a close, as the tide turned, she told herself, although she could not truly remember.

He stopped beside her, his masculine scent of safety and strength flaring her nostrils. "Do you want to go in?" He nodded towards the harbour.

She drew in a long breath, glanced longingly at the water. "There's a bath in the room?"

"Of course."

She allowed a sad smile to soften her features. "Then, no. It will suffice, for now."

He nodded, bit his lip and looked away. "Fresh water good, salt water better," he muttered.

So, she was not alone in re-visiting their memories. He was doing it, too. And his words immediately catapulted her back to the little cafe on one of the back streets of the old town of Barcelona where she had first uttered the words to him as she picked at the seafood from a paella and tried to explain the rules of her life to the wide-eyed boy before her.

"Fresh water is good," she had told him. "And always works in a crisis but salt water is my home and I need to return to it."

He had nodded, his naturally pale face darkened by freckles called forth by the glare of the Mediterranean sun. "Fresh water good, salt water better. Gotcha," he had repeated with his charming smile. "Then I guess we need to stay near the coast."

"Mostly."

They were quiet for a while and she noticed then that he was not eating his paella with his normal youthful gusto but chasing the food around the plate rather as was her own habit. "You don't like it?" she asked.

"I do," he replied but still did not eat.

She put down her fork and regarded him. The instant her gaze focused on him, a bloom of embarrassment further coloured his tanned face. Adam's apple bobbing nervously in his throat, he did not hold her stare but looked away towards the centre of the square, appearing to try to lose himself with fake interest in the tourists that milled there reading menus, taking photos or trying to find their wandering children.

"What's wrong, Bartek?" she asked, voice coated with honey and concern.

He gulped again, licked his lips, looked at her and away, as if holding her gaze brought him a physical pain, and cleared his throat with a cough. "It's just . . ." he began but his voice was at its most unsteady and so he stopped. He was looking down shyly now, twirling his napkin around his long fingers. "It's not that I haven't but . . ."

She reached out, took hold of his nervous hands and squeezed until they stopped twitching. "It's okay, Bartek," she said.

He was desperately avoiding eye contact. "I mean, I have but not . . . not like . . . with a lady like you." He stopped, drew in a shuddering breath and raising his eyes to pierce her gentle, supportive stare, he revealed ashamedly. "I don't think I can be the . . . uh . . . man you want me to be." His face was burning now with humiliation as a nervous chuckle followed swiftly behind the tumbling confession, the self-depreciating laugh that he used so often to cover his discomfort.

She squeezed his hands tighter and pulled him towards her. "You are exactly the man I need you to be. The universe has decided it."

She did not tell him any more at that point. Instead, she boosted his confidence and massaged his faltering ego, filling his mind with visions of the beautiful places she would show him, the wonderful time they would have together.

He would learn more later—that the act to which he was referring would never happen, that she needed the strength of his spirit, his unwavering devotion, and commitment. But what she did not want, did not need, indeed could not have, was any sort of sexual contact with a human. She shuddered at the very thought of it. It was against the very laws of nature.

Neither did she tell him that, as his binding to her grew stronger, his physical need would diminish until he would become as celibate and undemanding as the most cloistered monk locked away from the world with only his piety for company. Experience had taught her that telling such truths to her watcher at this early stage would only unsettle and undermine him.

He listened, transfixed, anguish apparently forgotten, hardly breathing, lost in the enticing net that she cast over him like the doomed fish caught by the inexorable sweep of the trawler. But to his credit, when she finally stopped, he said simply, "How?"

She was stunned. The question had never been asked before. Her watchers simply accepted what she said and lived with it, adapting themselves to fit the constricting straitjacket of service she expected them to wear. "How?" she repeated.

He nodded, gulped. That Adam's apple really was taking a beating today. "How do you pay, to do all this stuff? Do you have money?" As if to emphasise his point the waiter appeared and left the bill at the edge of the table, then backed away to return to his other customers.

"Money?" She chuckled at Bartek's naivety and then went on to describe to him the concept of psychic compulsion—the power she had over his species to transfer an idea into their head which they would then act upon. She even demonstrated it when the waiter returned and picked up the bill, smiled brightly and accepted no money as payment in full and mumbled his appreciation.

Bartek scowled and shuffled in his seat, clearly

uncomfortable.

Completely bewitched by his reaction, she suddenly felt the need to justify herself. "It's harmless. I get what I want and the person gets a shot of real satisfaction to their aura. I normally choose dickheads," she disclosed. "Businessmen who are screwing their secretaries, thieves who have stolen it from somebody else. In the scheme of things, it amounts to nothing and the world moves on. Really."

"What about the victim?" he asked.

"As I said I always choose—"

"The waiter?" he pressed, raising his eyebrows in the direction of the busy man rushing to serve his customers. "What happens when they do the books at the end of the day? He loses his job."

This was novel. She had never been challenged, never needed to vindicate herself, get defensive, with a watcher. "It's just a meal. He'll be fine. I can make sure the manager does nothing to him by using the same power."

But Bartek wasn't backing down. "What about the businessman's wife, his children? What about the person the thief stole from in the first place?" He shook his head sadly. "There's always a victim, unseen, voiceless, overlooked." His voice trembled. "Left alone to suffer."

Fala regarded him, as the realisation hit that she had never been a victim, never understood what it meant. She had simply dismissed such people as weak and useless. She had suffered much—lost her whole world, everything she had ever held dear, but she had always had the power to fight back, to defend herself.

The bitterness in Bartek's voice, the sudden slump in his shoulders, betrayed a whole lifetime of suffering and clearly indicated that he regarded himself as a victim.

She was struck then with how it must have been for him—a lonely boy growing up with no father or family, only a mother who was unable to love him as much as she loved the fictional characters on her television.

This was unnerving. Had she ever felt sympathy for her watcher at this early stage before? Frustrated, she could not remember doing so. She seemed to recall it normally came much later as the tide began to turn and their time together grew short.

Fala was silent for a long time, uneasy, not sure why this young man before her was different. She felt suddenly unstable, as if bobbing about on an erratic ocean and being unable to right herself. As she sought to explain it her rational side took over, quashing her misgivings, giving her a justification, a life jacket in the rough sea, which she grabbed willingly. Surely, it was a blessing that she had found him and she swore to herself, he would never feel so powerless again.

His moral compass had remained strong throughout the years, so much so that Fala believed he had never broken the law or taken advantage of anyone if he could possibly help it. He positively abhorred it when Fala used her psychic powers even for their own good, and would scowl distastefully, muttering about *doing things properly*.

She had changed her ways as a result, by not targeting individuals but institutions that could well afford it. But such actions were getting increasingly harder as the world was overtaken by non-human based systems. She knew G'llaha was somehow to blame for the sudden progress in e-technology and she could not fight it. It had a worrying effect on her, though. It was impossible to use psychic powers against a computer program.

She remembered that night in Barcelona well—possibly because it was the time when the true import of how his life had changed had begun to sink in.

Bartek, although still awed by the brilliance of her presence, had seemed distant and unhappy. They had walked through the marina, a silver moon reflected on the black waters, the heat of the day diminished but still warm enough to make a pleasant evening.

It was then he had revealed his disquiet.

"Tell me about Bartosz," he had said, his voice quiet but firm, as they gazed out across the water, lapping at the quay, calling her home.

Shocked, she had a real fight to stop the surprise showing on her face. *My, it was hard to remain inscrutable with this guy who missed nothing.* She cleared her throat, to give herself time to think of a reply that would satisfy him.

"Why?" It was the best she could do.

"We've been together for almost six months. You mention the others, well the recent ones anyway. You joke about their habits, you grow sad at their loss, you talk to me about them but you have never mentioned Bartosz."

"And what makes you think there even was a Bartosz?" She could not soften the testiness in her voice, couldn't appear unmoved although she tried.

Bartek smiled, a sad smile, far older than his years. "Sometimes, in your sleep, you . . ." He stopped, let the revelation hang to make its own way in the world.

Fala drew in a shocked breath, looked out to the sea as if it could rescue her from the embarrassment of this situation. Surely, she could not be as ill-disciplined as that? And yet, how would Bartek know the name if she wasn't?

Lies and half-truths flitted through her mind but in the end, she thought she owed Bartek the truth, if only because of what they would come to mean to each other.

"I don't mention him, it is true," she disclosed. "I don't want to set you against him." She reached across, ran her hand along Bartek's razored cheekbone and smiled with all of the strength she could muster. "See? The green like the kelp fields of Rannor swirls in your eyes already."

He raised his own hand, lifted it to cover hers and squeezed softly. "I'm not jealous. He is long gone and I am here. I need to know. Need to learn what he did to become your favourite. How he protected you. See if I can do better."

She moved their hands, brought them to her mouth and kissed his. Their eyes met. "I will tell you when the time is right. But not now. Now there is enough for you to learn without burdening your soul with my greatest failure."

He nodded curtly, accepting her vow.

But she had given him a gift that night—a present that bound him to her even more tightly, the same gift she had given all of her watchers at some point in their relationship—her father's knife.

It was a beautiful weapon. Made from the tusk of a narwhal, the shimmering blade had been fortified by impregnating the ten million tiny holes in its surface with the strongest material in the ocean, geothite, sourced from the teeth of limpets.

She remembered her father wielding the weapon with grim yet beautiful skill and could never control the wave of pride that washed through her at the memory.

He had given it to her on his deathbed, along with a secret she had shared with no one, when his talent for creating the most wonderful creatures had fritted away to bitterness. He had used the last of his strength to infuse the blade with long-lost mystic magic, to bind it to her so that it always found its way back to her.

Indeed, for a long time, its sudden return to her presence had been the sign that her watcher was no more, that he had given his life to protect her.

Bartek accepted the gift with awe and humble dignity and much disbelief. He had instantly set about learning all the things he must.

He had thrown himself diligently into a program that she designed for him. Selflessly, he had spent hours in the gym increasing his fitness and strength, attended numerous self-defence courses, learnt as much about weapons and their application as any self-respecting Black Ops agent and spent hours listening to her as she recounted the history of her people until he had become the man who now stood next to her on this quiet Aberdeen night.

He had become the man she would trust to save her life, at the cost of his own, when the time came.

And that time was very close.

The bleak stench of something rotting oozed through the firmament like sewage in a disused canal. It pulled her back to the road beside the harbour. Bartek stiffened beside her, reaching inside his winter coat for her father's narwhal knife he kept secreted there.

Fala perceived the gathering darkness as her senses returned and strengthened. She scanned the area eagerly.

"There!" she hissed.

On the road in front of them, the street lights flickered and dimmed and the traffic lights were stuck at red in every direction. Suddenly there were no cars or trucks to splash through the puddles at the side of the road, no people walking to the nearby gaudy shopping centre to be indignantly sprayed by the cold water. The world was empty.

A lone seagull the size of a cat, conducting a robust campaign against a MacDonalds wrapper in order to liberate a discarded piece of cheeseburger, let out a startled screech and leapt up into the sky, and not a moment too soon, for where it had stood, seemingly sucking the light and life out of the scene, a dark shape solidified into being.

Fala's heart began to throb in her chest as fear-fuelled adrenaline flooded excitedly around her body.

"Hooded murmurer," she breathed.

CHAPTER SEVEN

The murmurer stood halfway up Market Street, Christmas lights, golden stars, and green trees, flashing erratically making a bizarre backdrop. It looked down the hill at them, its hood cocked to one side as if in a pensive mood.

Fala had seen many and never failed to be impressed by their presence—it was a deep, hopeless black, as profoundly black as the wing of any crow, no hint of light seemed able to penetrate the infinite darkness, although it shimmered slightly like the picture on an old black and white TV screen, coming in and out of focus, there and not there, alive and yet not so. And all the time, like a dying star, it sucked in the energy around it, subsuming all with parasitic glee.

With real effort, Fala pulled her eyes away from its grotesque form and glanced across at Bartek, who was in full defensive mode, his jaw set firm and his blade, held tightly, glowing dully in the gathering gloom.

He turned to her, raised his eyebrows at her unspoken question but did not answer further. He was ready, whatever she should decide.

Feeling very old and tired, Fala drew in a long breath and glanced about her. The memory of the last cycle, thirteen long years ago, crashed into her mind, as unwelcome as a spring tide surging over coastal defences. This was where it had ended for her last watcher, dear sweet Kymani.

The past would not be denied entry into her consciousness and she closed her eyes for an instant to see again the shock in Kymani's naive, teardrop eyes as the knife of the bruiser dug deep into his guts. She saw his innocent blood, hitting the cold air, pooling to scarlet, as it gushed from his wound and stained the pavement.

Poor Kymani. He had tried but his genes had been weak, his strength flawed and for that he had died here, not even making it to the sacred waters to protect her during the ceremony.

She did not believe that Bartek was so feeble but still, protectively, she sent out a psychic scan to the surrounding area. She could sense no other malevolent presences save the murmurer. There appeared to be no nearby knife-wielding bruisers, intent on butchering her companion, and for that she was thankful.

The difference in the way this occasion played out from the last may mean nothing. G'llaha rarely employed the same tactics twice. She was thoroughly acquainted with the path to her destiny and she knew from tragic experience that although it may deviate a little, the overall destination always remained the same.

She opened her eyes.

The scene had not changed. It was waiting only for her to decide and she knew she really had no choice. The murmurer must be heard.

She stepped forward cautiously. Bartek remained, as if attached by an unseen thread, at her side, solid and seemingly indestructible.

How she wished that were true.

The murmurer let out a cackle of excitement like the crack of a whip as they neared. "Greetings, dear lady." It was the voice of her nightmares, deep, rich and evil. It sent a ripple of abhorrence tingling all the way down Fala's spine.

A sudden impatience, a need to have it all finished, grabbed at her and, forsaking all caution she snapped, "What do you want, G'llaha?"

The chuckle grew into a fully formed guttural laugh, oozing confidence and derision. "I think you know by now, Fala, or you really are pretty stupid."

Fala ignored the jibe, deciding attack was her best strategy. "There was a time you would not dare come to me like this."

"Indeed. There was a time when you were powerful enough to stop me, wasn't there? But not now. Now I may visit you as I please, although I offer my apologies for neglecting you for a while. I have been rather busy of late."

Fala let out an irritated, impatient *tut*.

"My, but you look so like your mother when you curl your pretty lips into a scowl. She scowls a lot these days, it's about all she can do. That and cry, of course!"

"Stop it!"

G'llaha ignored her and continued. "Your power is fading too, Fala. I know it and you know it. How many times must we complete the cycle? How many times must you cause suffering when the conclusion is obvious. You will be mine and I will have your secret. We are the only two left who are compatible."

"The cycle must be completed. Zuni will come." Fala worked hard to stay calm, to sound sure and to hide the doubt that threatened to seep through the seams of her belligerent assertion.

"Zuni?" The amusement in G'llaha's disembodied voice dripped like syrup from a spoon, the saccharine superiority of his words truly sickening. "He is long gone. Give yourself to me and let us stop this ridiculous waiting game. I am the only one worthy to be your mate."

"No."

The hood shook condescendingly. "Really, Fala."

"You expect me to give myself to you when I have seen what you have done to my brothers and sisters? You destroyed my people." Her calm was lost as the chaos of her emotion, her pain, took control. "You expect me to let you enslave me? Take my powers? Give me a child? It will be an abomination! I never will."

"But you will have to eventually, of course. So much better if you do it now before I overwhelm and destroy you entirely. You are alone. Your allies are weak."

Bartek stiffened beside her, straining, even more taut. He appeared to tremble, at the very edge of his tolerance. Fala could not help but glance over to him. She placed a reassuring hand on his shoulder.

G'llaha laughed. "He's like the others, Fala. You cannot rely on him. You think he is bound to you like in the old days but the ties are weak and loose, his genes diluted by the years. He will not protect you, he cannot, not like the others did in the past. He will fail and die like the other recent feeble souls and for what?"

"You know very well!"

"I know enough to offer you a truce. Surely you are as tired of the cycle as I am. What is so wrong with a peaceful solution? Saving lives? Your gadger doesn't need to die, not again. You can keep him as your pet if you like. Only join with me and stop the horror, once and for all. Together let us shape the future."

"You are the horror, G'llaha!"

"Me? You are being disingenuous again, Fala. Does your gadger know the truth, the price he has already paid and what he will pay again to ultimately settle your debt?"

"Shut up."

More laughter, exquisitely brutal and dripping with arrogance. "So, he doesn't. Oh, how delicious you are, Fala, princess of the seas! And you call me a horror! Shall I tell him? Does he not yet understand the nature of your relationship, the parasite you are? Abusive? It just doesn't cover the half of it, does it? Hasn't he begun to wonder why he feels so worn out, so used up, so empty all the time?" The voice droned on.

Fala's fear was growing, threatening to consume her in a wave of pure panic, like a huge breaker hitting the harbour wall. She had to stop him.

Secrets as old as time could not be revealed. Not like this . . .

She raised her hand as if to shield herself from his attack, biding time as she sought a reasoned defence through the fog of anger that clouded her mind but as she did so, miraculously the murmurer stopped talking and let out a high-pitched squeal.

The cloak folded in on itself and fluttered, empty of substance, to the pavement. It disintegrated as it hit the concrete and only a drizzle of thickening black wax remained to congeal on to the kerb, then decomposed further into grey ash to be blown away on the cold north wind.

Shocked, Fala looked at Bartek. His face was set in a resolute frown of distaste as he wiped the foul residue from his narwhal knife. "No hope is better than false hope," he muttered as he re-sheathed the dagger and turned back to their discarded bags further down the road.

Fala forced herself to relax.

She was tired. Her muscles throbbed painfully as she fought to retain this alien form and she longed for the rejuvenation that only the water in the harbour, so teasingly close, could bring. But she pulled herself together, forcing herself to move away from its seductive call, forced herself to carry on as she had always done.

As Bartek came up behind her, carrying their bags, she dejectedly shuffled up the hill, and made herself a monumental promise—once she was comfortable, she would finally tell her watcher everything. Not the story of her people which he already knew, but her own personal tale.

It was not how it had ever been in the past, she was sure. Her watchers had gone to their deaths ignorant of the role they played, never questioning their part in it, proud and content to serve her, to die for a cause they did not understand.

But she sensed, borne on the salty sea breeze, a huge change in the universe this time.

This time would be different from what had gone before.

She would not selfishly bind Bartek to his fate, as she had Kymani and Bartosz and all the others before. If he stayed with her, it would be his choice, not hers.

CHAPTER EIGHT

An hour later, following their check-in to the rooms Bartek had arranged and a long soak in a deep bath, Fala was re-thinking her earlier pledge. They were seated in a cosy craft beer bar beneath their rooms on the Gallowgate. Over the years Bartek had developed quite a taste for locally brewed beer, and he was sipping a pint of golden liquid now as he sat across the table from her and waited. Fala nibbled on a cracked pepper chip and sat back into the welcoming embrace of a saggy leather sofa in the corner of the bar, still unsure of her next move.

Outside the rain had come on. Drops splattered and ran lazily down the window beside where she sat. She pulled her gaze inside to regard her surroundings. This close to Christmas the bar was a hot, noisy refuge from the worsening weather. There were a handful of customers, regulars, who seemed content to be out of the rain and craved the luxury to chat softly and savour their beer and the deep *thud* of the bass of the CD that played had the soothing comfort of a mother's heartbeat to the child in her womb. But the rest of the place, drunk on strong beer and holiday cheer, was loud and wild, with jeers and laughter regularly jarring the senses.

Fala hesitated, wondering if her course of action was the best one. She knew from his quizzical look that Bartek sensed her unease, her unsettled indecision, and was correspondingly disturbed by it. It was so unusual for her to be so affected. She was normally so focused.

But she also knew he would not ask.

Still she vacillated.

It would be so easy to forget her vow, to simply go on as before, and in truth, Fala had been known to change her mind and her morals to benefit her own selfish need as often as a teenage pop diva changed her clothes. But this time something felt different. Fala reneging on her oath could only cause her guilt to bite deeper, and seemingly, and surprisingly, more important to her at that moment, Bartek deserved so much more from her. Had she learnt nothing from the tragedies she had left in her wake for centuries? Keeping her watchers ignorant had only ever ended badly. This time she would do the right thing.

So haltingly she began her story. "I will tell you why we are here."

Bartek snorted, drew back from her. "You don't—"

"Yes, I do." She cut across his protestation. "I promised you once I would tell you of Bartosz when the time was right. The time is now."

Bartek gulped, bit his lip nervously and looked away, but then he nodded in acceptance. He stood up, vacated his stool and moved to sit beside her on the couch. His closeness brought a further intimate heaviness to a moment that Fala was already having difficulty in shouldering but she pressed on.

"I know you believe I named you after him. That is partly true but there is another Bartek that I have known for centuries. Bartek is the given name of a famous ancient oak tree who grows in Zagnańsk near Kielce in the Świętokrzyskie Mountains of Poland. His age has recently been established to be six hundred eighty-seven years precisely." She sighed sorrowfully as the overbearing burden of her sad past threatened to crush her completely. "I didn't need the scientists that crawled all over him to tell me this because I was there when he was planted by a pretty little country girl with blonde braids and a sweet smile, so long ago. Now he is a mighty tree. He has withstood all storms, fire and famine, drought and danger, everything in fact that has assailed him. He remains a constant, standing proud and brave. So strong. He endures."

She sniffed and forced a smile. "I have returned to see him infrequently over the years. I was there when King Casimir III held his court under those beautiful branches and when King Jan III Sobieski rested beneath the canopy of lush leaves on his way back from the Battle of Vienna. Jan was a lad all right, he hid both a Turkish sabre and an arquebus plus a bottle of wine inside the massive trunk to commemorate his victory. Oh, how we danced under those bountiful leaves." Her smile strengthened as the memory warmed her heart, but then sadness chased the bloom from her cheeks.

"Bartek the oak is still alive, but he is in decline. His weakened trunk has begun to lean toward the heavy branches. Old age takes this most valiant of trees, as it will take all of us lucky enough to reach it one day. I have always been amazed by his silent strength, his fortitude and, in the hope that such attributes may inspire my young Polish sailor, it was after him I named Bartosz and so in a way you, too."

Bartek nodded but said nothing, truly captivated by her words.

"Do you want another drink?" The mood was somewhat fractured by the barmaid who stood beside their table. She was poured into impossibly tight jeans, in danger of bursting out of them at any minute, likewise straining sweatily around her ample curves a t-shirt gaudily emblazoned with the name of a local beer.

Bartek cleared his throat but still his voice was rusty with sentiment. "No, we're okay, thank you."

After the barmaid and her severely-under-duress clothes had shuffled away, Fala continued. "I have always loved the Baltic. For me, it is my home. I spent my youth there in our great citadel of Bothna at the centre of the Bothnian Sea between Sweden and Finland before G'llaha came to destroy it. It is in ruins now, only a few stones left but it was wondrous, and as a child, my playground was the whole of that beautiful region. I used to explore it with my friend Uznam with all the passion of the young." She stopped, sighed. "I have been back there often through my life. It holds the bittersweet memory of all that we once were and all that we lost."

She took a sip of her drink and Bartek mirrored her action with his own beer. "Bartosz was a sailor from Poland. He ran away from the political constrictions of his home at the age of sixteen, joined the deep-sea fleet." She passed her finger along the rim of her glass as she spoke. "He went overboard during a storm and was lost but of course he wasn't. I found him and saved him and helped him to fulfil his destiny."

She faltered, her face puzzled. "I am sure I have felt the same for other watchers down through history but time steals all sentiment, overlaying what once was with what now is. I cannot remember their features, not any of them, not clearly. There have been so many. When I think of them, I see only your face, my most recent watcher, and that is how it has always been. But Bartosz I remember because he was so perfect, and he almost succeeded in his impossible task. So different from those who have come since." She stopped, shook her head sadly. "Kymani and Arif, bless their souls, they tried, but the blood was weak in them. They never outshone the wonder of Bartosz."

She hesitated again, taking a sip from the glass of water. Bartek watched her acutely, moved closer to her so they were actually touching along the length of their bodies on the comfy sofa but he said nothing.

The door banged open and for a moment the warm life of the bar and the hypnotic thrall of Fala's haunting story were invaded by the harsh wind of a winter's night. But as the door slammed shut again just as quickly, Fala saw only a nondescript boy, wet hair plastered to his head and dripping past his already sodden hoodie to puddle on the threshold where he stood. He stepped forward, leaving a watery trail as he squelched past the shallow party people towards the bar.

Fala shuddered slightly, feeling a flux in the atmosphere of the place. She scanned the area but found nothing to fear, only the fleeting trace of something attractive and interesting. She dismissed it without further examination, too engrossed in her story. Now that she had started on the path she was determined to finish the journey.

"All the things you have surmised during our time together are true, Bartek. All the very worst things you laid awake at night and feared. I have used you, taken without asking, feasted on your energy, stolen your dreams. I should have told you, I should have at least asked your permission."

Bartek reached out to take her hands, his eyes burning brightly, holding hers in the most intense gaze. "Doesn't matter," he whispered hoarsely, and then a little stronger. "Without you I was nothing. I would give up on life before I give up on you." He squeezed her hands imploringly. "Finish the story, please."

"Very well," Fala nodded. "You know the cycle is a mating cycle. Every thirteen years I become fertile. I come to my spawning ground in the North Sea like the wild Atlantic salmon and I need to find my mate. In the past, I would have the pick of my people. There would be a great ceremony and we would rejoice. Oh, the joy. But since G'llaha destroyed them, the choice has become less and less until now only one merman remains, Zuni from the Pacific, to answer my call. He came that night and Bartosz managed to fight off G'llaha and his men on the shore, long enough for us to mate but, as with all things, even the act does not guarantee success."

She closed her eyes as the memory tore at her with sharp, ripping teeth. A dull pain throbbed at the centre of her forehead, as a hot flush washed through her. "Too soon G'llaha was in the water. We fought together, Zuni and me, against the Shape Shifter and his bruisers, water versus fire, a mighty battle, when the very sea boiled with our fury and the storm cracked the sky. At the end, I was left alone on the sea bed that had become our battlefield, littered with corpses of both friend and foe. Zuni swam away." She shuddered. "I can still hear his mournful cries. I fear he was fatally wounded. And G'llaha retreated. He was hurt, too, slinking back to his lair to lick his wounds, although his injuries were obviously not bad since he recovered soon enough to taunt me still."

"And Bartosz?" Bartek asked gently.

Fala sniffed, her eyes watering. "He drowned before I could get to him. I found him floating face down as the storm subsided and the sea relented. He was the first . . . the only one that I had seen . . ." She stopped, eyes moist, licked her lips. "For centuries before, I have lost count how many times I had lost my watcher on the final night of the cycle but I had never seen the actual consequence. They simply disappeared and eventually I found a replacement. This time I held Bartosz's lifeless body in my arms. I knew he was gone and he was never coming back." She hesitated again. "And I knew it was my fault. I saw the outcome of my action and I had to take responsibility for it."

Bartek squeezed her hands supportively. "He would not blame you, I know."

"But that does not make it right. Nor does the fact that after I lost him, I have gone on to do the same to two others, three if we count you."

"I am not dead yet," Bartek replied softly, although the granite strength at his core was evident in his voice. "There was no baby?"

"No." Fala shook her head too violently, her hair bobbing about her shoulders. "And the two times after Zuni has not returned. I fear that he is here no more and yet, it is not like the others I have lost. I can still sense his presence, weak, like a shadow of his former strength but still there. As we have travelled the world I have searched for him and his trace remains constant but so very fragile." She drew in a deep breath. "In my worst moments I fear. I fear that I am the only one left, the only one able to fight G'llaha and his nest of—"

As she finished the sentence, she pulled her eyes away from the sanctuary they had sought throughout the telling of the story in her watcher's fathomless stare and realised that another now sat on Bartek's vacated stool listening intently to the story.

The young boy who had entered earlier held her gaze. "What's my name?" he asked.

Shocked at his appearance and the fact that neither she or Bartek had noted his presence until this moment, her mouth finished the sentence her brain had already moved on from. "—vipers."

Magically, the whole firmament suddenly shifted as if it had released an unexpectedly deep sigh. Lights flickered, silence fell and hearts stopped for a second as a blanket of well-being fell over the whole building. Everything paused for a glorious moment, as if the universe took a well-deserved rest.

Then, a glass, untouched, tumbled to the floor behind the bar and shattered noisily. And with that the enchantment seemed to lift. The jovial buzz of chat returned, slightly cheerier than before and the bar staff, baffled, regarded the remains of the broken glass on the tiles before them.

"Vipers," the boy repeated with a hazy nod, blue eyes wide and receptive.

Belatedly Bartek, as if awoken from a deep slumber, lurched forward. "What the fuck just happened?" he demanded.

Fala shook her head in disbelief, looking from the boy to Bartek and back again. "My new watcher just arrived," she muttered.

"Your new—" Bartek was uncharacteristically aghast. "The hell? But I'm still here."

Fala gulped, her face ashen, her confusion evident. "This has never ever happened before," she muttered bleakly.

CHAPTER NINE

Fala closed her eyes as the ache in her forehead began to pulsate painfully. Her whole body was undergoing the change, preparing itself for what was to come. It was increasingly soul-sapping and exhausting to hold her human shape. She let out a long evocative sigh and forced the weariness and the pain away. Things would not get better any time soon.

Bartek gave her the tenderest of glances, taking his eyes off the country road that he drove down and, for his endless empathy, she threw him back an enigmatic smile.

On the back seat of the car where he was stretched out like a contented cat, Vipers, stupid name but there was nothing she could do about it now, let out a sleepy snort and rolled over but did not waken.

The thought of the kid turned her smile a little more sincere. Already she felt herself drawn to him. He was full of life and hope and—

But then her grin faded completely. The contrast between him and Bartek bit hard as she remembered her loyal watcher had once been like that, too—before she'd sucked it out of him.

They had stayed in the bar the night before until closing time, Vipers wolfing down three burgers and six cokes as if he had never eaten in his life before and he needed to fill every inch of his skinny body. It was true he would need the energy as the changes buried deep in his DNA began their work on him.

He had been animated, cute and boyish, asking so many questions, forcing them out along with the odd morsel of food through his ever-burger-full mouth.

In the end, he had asked one personal and ill-considered question too many. "So, you guys screwing, then?"

Bartek had growled at him from behind his pint glass. "Just shut the hell up!"

The kid had deflated instantly, like a balloon but without the *bang*, all of his cockiness vanishing, making himself small and insignificant as he cowered away from Bartek, obviously lost in muscle-memory that told him physical pain would follow the snarl.

Fala felt a wave of sadness as she wondered where the boy had come from, what violent horrors had stained his past for him to react like that but she didn't have time to ask, as Bartek, face darkening with self-reproach, realised by the kid's reaction he had overstepped some unseen mark.

"Look," he started apologetically. "There are two sorts of people in the world, kid—those that cause a fuss and those that just get on and do shit. Please, for the sake of my continued sanity, be the latter." It was a long speech for the increasingly taciturn watcher and Fala shifted her gaze to look at her longtime companion.

Her heart ached. They fit together so well. It had become easy for her to take him for granted, to expect selfless perfection from him every time she required it, but the sudden arrival of this new boy had rocked such foundation to its core.

Bartek's jaw was set firm but his face was pale in the dim bar light. He was holding it together. He would continue to do so, she knew, but what must be swirling around inside his head? How hard was it for him to carry on when he knew destiny was rushing towards him with the unstoppable force of an express train and his time was ending.

Not only that but the universe had seen to it that his replacement had already arrived.

She pulled her eyes away, banishing such thoughts, letting go of the guilt. It made her weak, made her lose conviction. She could not help Bartek, no matter how much she wanted to. It was better for them both. She had an improved chance of surviving if she did not use up her limited energy even trying.

But her culpability was strong. She had tasted it in the bar and she tasted it now, bitter as quinine in her mouth, as she looked across at him in the car. They had made a good team, one of the best, but its ending was coming soon.

They both had to accept it.

Their later years together had been good, built on mutual trust and his unfailing loyalty but it had not always been so. A searing memory cut through her consciousness, so sharp, vivid as the most expensive HDTV image, and she could do nothing but sit back and watch it.

They were in Melbourne, Australia, the first year of their partnership.

Travelling had always been difficult for Fala. She could and should have been able to swim anywhere but that was not a valid option anymore.

Each time she entered the sea water it set off a psychic boom, undetectable to humans with their limited perceptions, but vibrating through the firmament, a squeal of pure wonder that she, one of the last of her people, had returned to her home. The boom brought marine animals from far and wide to celebrate with her which was an utter joy.

What was not so helpful was the fact that G'llaha and his minions heard it, too, and could pinpoint her location instantly. For that reason, her trips into the briny water that gave her life had to be limited and rushed. She could swim for a while and luxuriate in the peace it gave her but long distances were out of the question.

Still, she had to keep moving. Cars and trains were adequate for short journeys but could not take her to different continents as she frantically sought to stay ahead of her pursuers.

Remembering the freedom of the iconic sailing boats of centuries before, she had tried cruising on the big hotel ships that now ruled the seas but that had turned into a living hell—so close to the sea but unable to dive into it whenever she wanted because of eagle-eyed seamen who would cry "Man overboard," launching boats to rescue her. And even if they did not, she had no means of getting back on the ship.

It was far too much hassle.

With no bath in her cabin, she had had to resort to sneaking into the swimming pools in the middle of the night when the need got just too strong to endure, ducking under the water and allowing her tail to soak in the barely satisfactory chlorinated water.

Aircraft were quicker and therefore better but she never knew when the need would take her. She remembered a particular flight to Melbourne from Madrid that had been hell. As the rest of the plane had slept, the need had bitten so deep she had no hope to control it. She had struggled to the toilet after waking Bartek and he had followed a few minutes later.

She still recalled her complete humiliation at the knowing look the grey and crumple-suited businessman sitting in an aisle seat, his company obviously valuing him only at economy level, had thrown her as they returned to their own seat long minutes later, his smutty idea of what had been going on written all over his lecherous face. The truth had been far different from the mile-high club he envisaged—the overwhelming smell of barnacles and brine, Fala sitting on the toilet, her tail stretched out and Bartek, squashed in between her and the pathetic sink, swearing profusely, trying desperately to lubricate her scales by pouring water over them from a paper cup.

It had been truly horrible, as had the keeping of her human form as they queued through Immigration Control, and when they finally made it to their hotel, Fala had no energy left to do anything but lay in a bath for hours and let her weary muscles relax in their original form.

She remembered waking up and finally feeling almost normal again. But the contentment did not last long. For the first time since she had met him, Bartek was not there.

The room was dark and empty, their bags thrown in the corner, the remains of a room service meal, meat of course, discarded on a plate on the table.

Her alarm vibrated through her.

Something was wrong.

She dressed quickly, throwing on jeans and a t-shirt as she glanced at the clock to see it was almost midnight. She could find him easily enough. His psychic presence beamed out of the firmament at her, like a lighthouse on a dark night. What she didn't understand was why he wasn't at her side, caring for her, as was his responsibility.

He knew how devastated she was from the journey and yet he had abandoned her. Doubts rose in her mind once more. Was he not the one? Or worse still was he so genetically flawed, so weak, that he could not fully fulfil his role? Could he not look after her as he should, as she deserved?

These thoughts whirled around her mind as she made her way down to reception. When they had checked in, she had been barely clinging on, almost out of it, as the need tortured her but now, on recollection, she remembered the girl behind the counter. The way she had looked at Bartek, rolled her eyes, flirted with him and even more worryingly, the way he had responded—smiling beautifully, his long fingers lingering on her hand as she gave him the key, all confidence and swagger—like a young buck in his first mating season.

How could she have missed the attraction? And what did it mean? Fala had never had a watcher stray in such a way before. The odd soulful glance at a pretty girl, the black dog of depression that she had had to chase away, or a fall into desperate monosyllabic introversion were the normal negative reactions she had dealt with in the past.

Fala pictured the girl, dark and petite with the most beautiful deep autumn brown eyes and an obvious penchant for tight, short skirts, her shapely thighs visible when she turned to reach for the electronic room key. Fala sensed now, in retrospect, that what the girl lacked in size, she made up for in her sheer voluminous personality that entered a room a good minute before the rest of her.

A sharp sliver of jealousy, an emotion she had seldom had the need to feel before, pierced Fala's consciousness as she walked out of the hotel's sliding doors into the night to follow Bartek's psychic trail.

The sky was dark but the man-made city lights beamed out effortlessly to nullify and brighten the sinister shadows. Fala made her way down past Flinders Street Station and over the river. To her left, majestic and arrogant on the hill, snoozing on past glories, the floodlit MCG. Softer, smaller lights twinkled in the trees that stood sentry along the banks of the Yarra River where the pretty young people played in the bars and restaurants, spilling out onto the boardwalk in a wave of excited chatter, punctuated by cigarette smoke and laughter.

The night air throbbed with the bass beat, feral and erotic, soaked in pheromones as thousands of bodies quivered like animals before a storm. The sheer intensity of the place, the energy, the promise of unimagined satisfaction, was almost too much for Fala to cope with, and she hesitated on the bridge steps.

Such pure human lust was something she had shied away from in the past but even she could not fail to be impressed by the untamed power that these human creatures could generate. There was something alluring and bestial in the lithe young bodies, the electricity that sparked between them as they touched and parted, laughed and chatted, easy and innocent but capable of such sin.

It made Fala sad.

She recalled her own folk, drunk on their own complacent importance, how badly that had ended, and she knew that G'llaha had similar plans to harvest the raw power of the human condition. Indeed, he was doing so already and was using the yield to change the planet for his own ends.

She pushed her doubts aside. Now was not the time.

Instead, she made her way along the vibrant river walk. Columns of flame spurted hot and vast into the night sky from outside the casino on the hour, buskers with amps to rival most small arenas boomed out an ever-thumping heartbeat of the night, and the heady sexual desire she had sensed earlier continued to ooze blatantly in the very air.

Even in this seething mass of humanity, it did not take her long to find her Bartek. He was sitting on a high stool at a table on the terrace of one of the bars. From inside the frantic strains of the DJ's sound system boomed out to override the excited chatter of the clientele.

Bartek was sipping a beer and in the instant Fala saw him he looked strangely unfamiliar, young and so very beautiful.

He had slicked back his hair, shaved the fuzzy whiskers from his chin, was wearing a new starched white shirt with too many buttons undone to teasingly reveal the top of his tanned chest. The pupils of his brilliant blue eyes were so wide they looked like a mesmerising dark chasm into which any woman would delight to fall.

Fala hesitated again.

Her feelings crashed through her with terrifying force. This was all wrong. She should not be here. She felt sure she should not need to do this. She had never needed to do it before. She felt incredibly uncomfortable and simply wanted to leave.

This place and its potential disconcerted her more than anything else had for a very long time but she would not give him up.

He was her watcher.

He was the one. She knew that with a clanging certainty deep in her soul. No trashy Australian dwarf with skirts disappearing up her own ass would take him from her. And that was truth.

But neither would she reduce herself to fighting, in a place like this. She remembered a scene from her youth when she and Uznam had lingered in the water just off the dock, completely fascinated at the sheer idiotic spectacle as two enormous fishwives screamed and scratched at each other over a drunken sailor laying senseless in the gutter nearby.

It had been so unbecoming, so pathetic, that they had laughed and shaken their heads at the foolishness of humans. Was that any way to behave to win a mate, really? Fala had been carved from the finest marble with class and dignity, painstakingly sculptured from pure finesse.

There would be no such scene from her.

Taking a deep breath and with great poise, she climbed the steps, ignoring the fear in her heart, forcing her rebelliously shaking legs to still, and made her way to stand before the table. People nearby, attracted by the obvious promise of drama, stopped talking and focused on the action.

The girl was sitting so close to Bartek that she was practically on the same stool and was rubbing her hand between his legs. Bartek's eyes were closed and he looked completely relaxed, resting his head on the girl's shoulder, at peace in a way Fala had never seen him before.

As Fala stopped before them, the girl ceased her rubbing and looked up at the newcomer.

"Oh hi," she said somewhat uncertainly, her cherry red lips cracking into an apprehensive frown as if she sensed danger. "Do you want something?"

"Yes, I do," Fala responded, injecting just the right amount of psychic dread into her voice.

Awkward wasn't a strong enough word to describe the sudden temperature drop around them. The healthy conversations withered and died as if they had been exposed to a thoroughly toxic chemical. Fala felt like everyone in the whole establishment was staring at them.

Bartek's eyes flashed open in panic. He at least had the decency to flush with embarrassment as he became aware of her presence. He stood up, dumping the girl on to the floor and knocking over his drink. The smash as the glass shattered into a thousand crystal pieces and threw beer over a number of feet in the vicinity attracted even more unwanted attention.

"Fala." He muttered, horrified. "I thought—"

The girl looked up at him, shocked eyes wide with questions but asking none of them. Somebody giggled, uncomfortable and nervous, others looked away, unable to stand the cringe-worthy tension.

In contrast, Fala enjoyed the scene. Her anger was hot and so delicious that she was disinclined to move. It rushed through her with tremendous power and for a moment she understood the emotion of those furious fishwives from long ago. She was breathing hard, staring at him as if she would find the answer to all of her own difficult questions by making a thorough analysis of his face. Unable to stand still, as the fury buzzed through her, she oscillated on the spot from one foot to the other and back again.

Formidable and frightening.

It was intoxicating to let the rage rule her but she rode it with the skill of a champion surfer on the big wave as, stepping forward, she raised her hand and slapped Bartek's face, hard. His head snapped back but she did not care. Turning on her heel, she left the place, ignoring the jibes that followed her.

"Jesus mate, your ma come to get you?"

"Bloody hell, that's quite a right hook, love."

"You betcha. Get in there, darling."

"Fair play, son, you had it coming."

She did not look back but she knew Bartek would be standing, staring, rubbing the welt burning on his cheek with his hand, tears of regret and mortification shining in his eyes.

She extinguished the vision, expunging him from her mind and continued the trek along the river bank, assertively pushing her way through the revellers, past the many bridges that spanned the river, until the bars finally thinned and changed to impersonal high-rise apartment blocks, the manmade lights were no more and the silent, natural darkness engulfed her.

A cold wind from the sea blew on the empty-hearted, far from the bright lights and vacuous laughter, down near the docks where the Yarra finished its long journey.

Fala removed her clothing, folded them neatly, left them on the dock and eased her body into the brown river water made thick with suspended clay, clumping as it mixed with the marine salts washed up from the ocean.

The relief was immediate and exquisite as the sea welcomed her, claiming her as one of its own and relaxing her. Her anger and disappointment floated away on the strong current.

She swam a long way out into the Bass Strait that night. Two bottle-nosed dolphins, Tim and Tam from the Baruwaluwu clan, beautiful creatures sleek and sure in the water, came to offer fealty to the last princess of the sea. With the benefit of their shared communal memory, they gleefully told her their ancestors had swum with her before and they were blessed to have the opportunity to do so, too. It was always nice to renew old ties and Fala begrudged them nothing.

They were playful and supportive. Sensing her disquiet, they forsook their regular bream fishing to accompany her. They frolicked long into the night, diving low and jumping high, and Fala felt her soul calming and her heart easing.

Sometimes one needed to let the universe simply find its own course.

All would be well.

As the weak dawn light inched over the horizon, Fala bade farewell to the dolphins and, returning to her clothes, was not surprised to see the silhouette of a lonely figure waiting for her. She accepted his hand as he pulled her from the water and enveloped her in a fluffy cotton towel.

"I'm sorry," Bartek sniffed, contrite. "Something pulled me to her. I don't understand."

She looked at him then and even in the weak light she could see the right side of his face was misshapen, his eye swollen and blackening, and dried blood was caked around his nose and staining the perfect white of his shirt. Surely she hadn't hit him that hard.

"What happened?" she asked.

They sat on one of the metal seats at the water's edge. Bartek gulped, his voice raspy and unsure as he began. "I went back with Evie. I shouldn't have, I know. I just wanted . . . I thought that . . ." He shrugged and gulped some more.

"It can never be, Bartek," Fala said softly.

His face crumpled in despair. "But I didn't choose this."

"It chose you, my darling, and neither of us can change it."

Then the silence came down, dense and impenetrable, like a widow's black veil, hanging between them. He was breathing heavily, sniffing back tears, nose blocked, trying to get enough oxygen into his struggling system. She just stared at him, waiting for the surge of words she knew would come.

They sat in silence for a long time. A lone seagull rode the circling air currents above and let out the loneliest cry. Bartek was still reluctant to speak. He shuddered beside her and Fala wondered how much of that was from adrenaline and fear and how much from the guilty realisation of his part in the events of the night. Very slowly she drew off most of his redundant emotion, feasted on it until she felt well-nourished following her swimming exertions.

Finally, she had calmed him down enough and he began again. "Bruisers came. Looking for you. They hurt-they hurt Evie-and I couldn't help her." He flexed his hands impotently. Fala saw that there was blood caked under his nails and his knuckles were bruised. "I tried to fight but there were too many. Evie screamed. I—" He stopped, shook his head, the memory obviously too raw to recount.

"Is she all right?" Fala asked, prepared to be magnanimous in victory. *Hot-headed and short-skirted she may be, but little Evie hadn't deserved what had befallen her.*

"I ran and they followed me. Caught me in an alley . . ." Bartek was shaking again and Fala took hold of his hands, squeezed them lovingly.

He turned to her. "Didn't tell them anything so they beat me until it all went black." He pulled back a hand, wiped it along the bubble of blood newly awakened by the telling and dribbling from his nose. "I went back to check. She wouldn't talk to me but I think she was okay. Just scared."

He extricated himself from Fala's grip, stood up, and

moved to the edge of the water. His shirt was ripped down the side and Fala could see a dark shadow bruising above his kidney and around to his ribs.

"I didn't mean for any of this to happen. I just felt compelled . . ." He halted, miserable and empty. His energy along with his emotion had been sucked away. He looked like he would give up and jump into the water at any moment.

Fala pulled the towel about herself and moved to stand behind him. She reached out to reassure him, to let her touch return a little of the energy she had stolen from him, to give him back his hope and his purpose. "I know you didn't, Bartek, but you have to understand. It's not like it was before for you. You have me now but in having me you have to renounce everything else. Give it all up. Let it go. It's just you and me now, forever."

His sniff was a shudder, deep and desolate, as he turned back to her. His eyes, pupils still huge, twinkled with tears in the grey light. Behind them, on the river, the dawn rowers skulled silently past, in the distance the reversing alarm of an early delivery truck squawked, and overhead a jetliner, its engines' roar for a moment eclipsing everything else, began its final descent towards the airport as the city woke for a new day.

"I understand." Bartek had replied solemnly.

Knowing that there were bruisers looking for them, they had left Melbourne soon after, travelling north. Fala recalled how Bartek had loved Australia. "The beer is cold, the weather is hot and they drive on the right side of the road. What's not to like?" He had finished the pronouncement with his trademark chuckle, and she had hoped the Evie escapade was forgotten.

They decided to try shorter flights following the near disaster on the trans-continental one and transited through

Melbourne many months later. And in the departure lounge, a discarded local paper had brought it all back.

Fourth Junkie found dead, the headline screamed, but what drew Bartek to pick up the inky rag was the picture of the pretty brunette, obviously from better times, below the words.

"Evie?" he breathed in disbelief.

He read the story, hands shaking, falling over the words, shoulders slumped with guilt, as Fala sat beside him and listened with growing disquiet. It appeared the young girl had overdosed on a hit from a suspected heroin batch that had already claimed three young lives in the past week.

The journalist, who had never met her, used all his powerful prose to wax lyrical about the tragic loss but didn't quite manage to infuse a sense of sympathy, even though this story was made so much more tragic by the fact that, up until eight months before, the victim had held down a good job and been well-liked within her large circle of friends.

However, after a traumatic and violent incident at her home, Evie Fabienne had spiralled downward into a chasm of hopelessness and despair with horrifying speed, falling from grace to die alone and unloved, caked in her own vomit, on the putrid floor of a Melbourne crack house.

There were quotes from her parents and friends but Bartek didn't read them. He stopped, bit his lip and gulped, wide eyes turning to Fala for an explanation she could not give.

She hugged him close, feeling the enticing power of his desolation. "I did that," he moaned.

"No, you didn't." She soothed him as best she could, rubbing his back supportively and whispering strength back into him with the patient tenderness of a lover.

He had gone totally silent and they had boarded the plane to Perth not long after. Morose for the following days, he never mentioned the incident again but Fala knew him well enough to know he had never forgotten it but carried it deep inside, locked away in the withering place he held all his mistakes.

Now, bumping along the frost-cracked road in the north of Scotland, Fala could not help feeling the same irritating itch she had felt long ago in that Melbourne departure lounge—that the universe was trying to tell her something, but she was damned if she could work out what it was.

CHAPTER TEN

The sky in this part of the world was big—so big it filled the eyes and overwhelmed the mind. Fala thought it every time she came here. Not only that, but it seemed to be greater than the one consistent whole that formed the ceiling of the rest of the planet.

Here it had seemingly separate parts. Behind them over Aberdeen it was grey, the rolling mist of the haar having claimed the beauty of the formidable granite buildings while in front, over the mighty Grampian mountains, it was effervescent, swirling dark blue and angry with the makings of a snowy storm. Above them, as they progressed along the narrow lane locals in these parts optimistically called a road, it remained for a while at least, amazingly benign, the bright blue innocence of a newborn's eyes. And yet it was all the same sky and the darkness of night loitering at its edge, waiting to swoop in from the east, threatened no mercy as it sought to engulf everything.

They had left the coast. Bartek had let his eyebrows rise quizzically at her command to follow the Inverness road northwest towards the mountains but he had said nothing and simply complied. The road had got increasingly worse and recently the jolting had ripped Vipers awake from his slumber. After complaining of being hungry, which seemed to be an ever-present problem with him, Bartek had thrown him a chocolate bar. The kid had eaten sullenly in the back, nose making a smudge on the window where he had pressed it as he gazed out at the passing land.

Fala's stare followed the boy's gaze. It was mostly undulating fields, the foothills of the mountains. Below the tree line, a patchwork of grey and brown ribbons was threaded through sparingly with blazes of vivid evergreen and above it, the heather, dark beneath its white winter coat, slumbering silently.

Fala had spent much time here with the farming communities of the area. She knew the soil was gravel and clay, good for rearing livestock, and they passed many Aberdeen Angus cattle, herded together for warmth, steamy breath hanging on the cold air and also woolly sheep muffled against the chill, feasting on the fingers of hardy highland grass poking out through the frost, grass that was never quite as green as that found further south.

Other fields were filled with winter wheat and one still contained the cylindrical bales of hay from the harvest, the land's last memory of a long-gone summer, left in a haphazard pattern. Fala fancied some giant having amused himself for a while by tossing his tubular toys about, had grown bored and moved off, forsaking them without a second thought.

They passed through a hamlet snoozing under the cover of fragrant lazy wood smoke, sheltered roofs whitened by the sugar coating of frost, still not melted by a winter sun that found it difficult to climb even halfway up the sky at this time of year.

To their left the three peaks of Bennachie, cloaked in snow, rose majestically as if in solar competition. Fala knew it was easy to be seduced by the sheer commonplace beauty of the scene, to feel secure in the wave of Christmas cheer that beamed through the inconsistent daylight from the flashing fairy lights of the houses and the big tree erected in the village square.

Travelling on, they crossed the railway bridge and their

destination came in sight. Watching over the next small town that had grown up beneath its roots, the small conical shaped hill called Dunnideer with its stone arch, stood out bravely in the gathering gloom.

They passed under a squad of stark silver-barked beech trees guarding the lane which, in warmer months, would have created a verdant, green tunnel but were now only bare, bereft branches lamenting their loss as they reached forlornly to each other across the road, like children ripped from their mothers, never again quite able to touch the comfort so close. On the track beneath, the bronze leaves of last year were piled in the gutter, decaying silently from brown to black to mush.

Bartek stopped the car in the pull-off below Dunnideer where Fala directed, still not asking any questions, but Vipers was not so circumspect.

"What are we doing here?" he asked.

Fala ignored him and, opening the car door, slowly moved her heavy legs to get out. The rush of freezing air stole her breath for a moment but she forced herself to look up, her eyes fixing firmly on the hill summit.

"You're not going up there." It wasn't a question that Bartek asked but a statement of fact.

Fala snorted to hide her surprise at his words. When had it become his place to tell her what to do? She ignored the urge to argue with him and simply responded, "I need to." She smiled tightly. "It is a sacred place. My secret place. I need to pay my respects."

"Can't you do that from here?" Vipers whined. "It's bloody cold out there."

Without another word, Bartek exited the car, slammed his door and moved around to Fala's side to help her out. Vipers swore when it became obvious that she was going up the hill but climbed out of the pleasant cocoon he had built on the back seat, and stood expectantly, waiting to serve, but not sure how or why, shivering in his thin hoodie and jeans.

The climb was not hard to begin with and, although out of breath, Fala made it to the rickety gate halfway up but from there the hill steepened considerably. The frozen grass became slippery and was peppered with treacherous rabbit holes. She hesitated, breath in the cold air suddenly difficult to come by, lungs labouring and heart struggling.

There was movement behind her. In the time it took to turn, without words, Bartek lifted her into his arms and, carrying her, steadfastly resumed his climb. She put her arms around his neck and laid her head on his shoulder.

She fit perfectly.

He was so strong, so willing. Even after all she had taken from him, she knew he was prepared to give so much more. Although she would not admit it, even to herself, she adored him at that moment with all the doomed passion of a teenage girl falling head over heels into her first love affair.

When they reached the top, Fala could feel the strain thrumming through Bartek's muscles, see the beads of sweat pooling in the worry lines of his high forehead below the beanie that was rakishly pushed back on his head. It had taken a lot out of him but he made no complaint, simply gulped in air and said nothing as he gently placed her on her feet before the stone arch, his hands lingering on her waist as if in an effort to continue their intimacy.

Fala waited for her legs to find the strength to bear her weight once more. She looked up at the familiar scene before her. On closer look, it was not an arch that topped the hill at all but the one remaining stone wall of a building from long ago, punctuated halfway up by what was once a window which from afar gave it its arched appearance.

Fala hobbled painfully to the wall. She reached out and ran her hand along the uneven stonework. "I remember when they built it," she murmured softly. "In your year 1265, a single rectangular tower, draughty and smelly, smoke always in your eyes, but a home, nevertheless." Her voice drifted, borne away on the cold northly.

"How could you possibly—" Vipers began from where he stood behind them.

Bartek silenced him by throwing a menacing look over his shoulder.

Fala wobbled slightly and leaned on the old wall for support as she continued, "Walls two feet thick but they still didn't keep out the stinging cold." She shuddered. "Of course, it wasn't the first dwelling here, nowhere near. I first came here in what you call the Iron Age at the same time as the first beech trees began to grow, just saplings then, following the route of the chattering streams below, when the Taexali people built a hill fort on this very spot." She sniffed, shook her head.

"I can still smell the wood smoke, the ash, the heat that caused my cheeks to burn. They stacked the rocks up over there, dry, no mortar but then they built up the timber around it and lit it. The heat was so intense it fused the rocks together into a solid surface. You can still see the effect there. See, where the native white rocks are embedded with a sort of darker asphalt? Vitrification, your people, with their need to quantify and classify all things, named the process."

Interested despite himself, Vipers moved to where she had pointed and ran his stained and split trainers over the glassy rock. "Why did they do it?" he asked. "Defence? Stronger walls?"

"In a way. They lived on the coast in the city of Devana, at the mouth of the River Dee where Aberdeen now stands." She waved her hand eastwards to where the grey sea haar enveloped the current city. "But this, this was their sacred place. They built the wall to protect it, to sanctify the area, to keep out the evil demons and allow their people to rest in peace."

"A burial place?" Vipers asked, curiosity chasing his teenage angst away.

Fala felt Bartek stiffen beside her. She turned towards him, eyes full of sympathy, and taking hold of his hand, led him around the arch to the other side of the hill where the wind was raw. The nettles that must have covered the area in the summer months had died out and three weathered earth mounds could clearly be seen clinging to the grassy knoll.

"The sea killed Bartosz, the sea and me." Fala's voice was strained as she sensed the emotion coursing through Bartek. She nodded nervously towards the furthest, smallest mound. "So, I brought him here away from the waves and the water to the safety of the land. They were a good people, the Taexali. I feel their presence still on the wind, engrained in the rock. Their spirit is here. They look after him. I brought the two that followed, Kymani and Arif, here, too."

Bartek straightened, stepped back and snatched his hand from hers. "It's as good as any place," he sniffed, shoving his hand deep into his pocket, disengaging, getting as close as he ever had to running away from her.

She nodded, trying to understand the deep currents that swirled within him, the anguish that washed across his face.

"Better than most," she agreed. "The Taexali believed that those buried here would not just be kept safe from the evil spirits of the world but that they would wait until they were needed again. Then, they would rise."

Bartek said nothing. He was shivering and Fala knew it wasn't from the cold wind.

She let out a humourless laugh, masking her desperation as she looked for a way to reach him, to make things right. This was not going at all as she had planned when she decided to come this way. "Well, we need them now," she finished inadequately, feeling more discomfort in his presence than she ever had.

"You can't be serious." Vipers, the churlish teenager once more, cut through the throbbing tension that had grown between the other two with the tactlessness of youth. "You couldn't walk up here on your own and you expect us to believe you carried up these guys up and buried them here?"

Fala pulled her eyes from Bartek's pale, stretched face and turned to the young man. "Nothing is what it seems, my dear." She sighed unhappily, fearing to go on but knowing she must. "I had help. People, particularly men, tend to do what I ask."

At her words, Bartek reacted as she knew he would. His whole body went rigid and his eyes flashed to find hers. He held her gaze for long seconds and then, snorting and shaking his head with frustration, he pushed past her, stalking away across the hilltop.

Vipers watched him go, eyebrows raised, but said nothing.

Fala held her breath she had been holding for long moments. Then, exhaling, she turned her eyes back to the ancient wall before her. She ran her hand along the rough stone, feeling the history that dwelt beneath, trying to find her equilibrium as her world rocked like an ocean liner in a hurricane.

"I once knew a boy," she began. "Who used to think that the gap above us was a gateway to another world. That we could step through and everything would be well."

"And is it?"

Fala smiled. "I wish."

They stood in silence, the wind whistling through the hole above them and slapping hard at the wall. Vipers, full of curiosity and query and unable to stop it brimming out, asked, "What was his name?"

Fala appeared distracted, glancing over her shoulder to where the grim figure of Bartek loitered. "Who?"

"The boy." Vipers let a hint of irritation colour his response.

Fala shook her head as if to clear it. Every sinew in her body wanted to go to her reeling watcher, wanted to soothe him, share his pain, but her pride stopped her. Instead, she ignored him. Focusing on her new boy was where the future lay. "William. His name was William and I knew him a long time ago."

"What happened to him?"

Fala turned back to the young man, reached out and ran her hand along his cold cheek. "What happens to every boy," she mused wistfully.

"I don't understand any of this," Vipers said despondently, his features curling into a scowl.

"No, you don't."

Fala moved away from him, to where Bartek stood. Vipers was perceptive enough not to follow her but instead took an interest in the stonework, running his hand along it as he had just seen Fala do, as if that would give him the answers to all the questions burning in his head.

"I have lived a very long time," Fala began, standing behind Bartek as he gazed out over the quilted Aberdeenshire countryside. A hawk, lonely and brave, rose up from the line of trees below them and swooped away to the north. Even higher, a plane drew a perfect saltire in the blue sky as it crossed the vapour trail from another flight. The sound of children playing below drifted up to them, louder than expected in the clean, fresh air.

The longing to make things right grew in Fala's soul. A need to make him understand. "I had seen everything there was to see and grown weary but you made me see it all anew through your eyes. You made me remember the wonder of it all, Bartek. You made me young again."

Bartek swallowed hard but refused to turn. "I bet you say that to all the boys," he said, voice grating, but there was no spite in his words, only a numbing sorrow.

"I have lived a long time with you humans and yet, it appears, I get it wrong sometimes still," Fala responded. No answer. "I'm trying to apologise," she said bluntly.

At her words, Bartek shuddered but did not turn. "Well, this must be a first."

"You are special. The only one I have brought here and it wasn't to cause you suffering, although I see now that has been the result."

"Then what did you bring me here for?"

"To show you there is a place for you, my secret, a place where you can be at peace."

"A piece of shitty ground on a Scottish hill. Am I supposed to feel grateful?" Bartek flexed his hands impotently. "A thousand years, god knows how many souls sacrificed for you. I bet you can't remember any of their names, and you still don't understand."

Fala stepped back from the uncharacteristic bitterness now darkening Bartek's voice, the dangerous violence of his stillness, the utter fury at his own predicament, and her bewilderment grew.

Disbelief flashed through her. *This did not happen.*

Granted, she had never revealed as much to any other watcher as she had showed him but never had they reacted with such resentful venom. They had not needed to understand or consider their own feelings. In fact, she was not sure they had even had any by this late stage. They had simply done as she commanded.

She was the important one in this.

They were disposable.

So, what was different this time, and why did it hurt so much?

She felt tears, frozen on conception by the wind, spring into her eyes. A deep desperate bloom of fear fractured her heart, quaking her hitherto unshakeable confidence. Where was his anger, his emotion, coming from? Why was he different? And from that, her thoughts spiralled downwards. Was he going to leave her? Could he? Was he going to walk away? Was that why the universe had given her Vipers so soon? What would she do if he did leave? How could she fight G'llaha with only Vipers? Where did it leave her?

All this dread bombarded her, this new feeling making her reel like she tottered on the very chasm of failure. She could not recall its like before but she pushed away her need to be first and tried instead to concentrate on the man before her, to understand how he must feel. To be there for him like he had been for her in so many ways over the last ten years.

"I don't want it to end like this," she said softly, reaching out a trembling hand to take hold of his shoulder.

Finally, he did turn to her, gulping, his eyes wide and shining as he took a deep, shuddering breath. Emotions, pure and strong and delicious washed across his features with the frequency of destructive waves on an eroding beach but slowing as if the storm was passing. Soon, he was calmer, the man she knew, the man she trusted to do what was necessary, and yet he was sadder somehow, as he said, "It will end for the best for you, Fala. It always does."

She was silent, letting the full import of his own words sink in, searching but failing to find a suitable response, knowing she could tell him no more.

"Come on," he said eventually, letting the rigidity in his body slacken and gravitating toward her. "Let me carry you down. Time is drawing on. We are losing the light and you have an appointment to keep. Zuni is waiting."

His outburst had upset her more than she cared to admit but she pushed away her fears with the deflective skill of a master, forced a smile and responded, "If only it were true."

CHAPTER ELEVEN

Fala drew in a deep breath. The car smelt of sugar and spice and all things nice.

Much to her relief, there were no plastic yellow arches or drive-thrus in this part of the world, so they had stopped at the village bakery instead.

Colourful winter pansies with brave faces painted white by the frost peeked out of the window boxes that surrounded the doorway. Shiny tinsel draped around the old-fashioned till and the large, cheery lady behind the counter had cheeks the same colour as holly berries. Like Vipers, she spoke with the soft, lazy burr of the area, slurring any number of words into one and she laughed like the rumble of an ancient steam engine. A merry old soul, she obviously enjoyed her work and she simply could not do enough for them.

Fala nibbled on a rich cinnamon bun and sipped at her hot chocolate as they started the journey back to the coast. Vipers had taken every single donut in the shop along with three large bottles of coke and was slurping away happily on the back seat. He had been more than annoyed when Bartek removed his iPhone from him the previous evening and dumped it in the trash, but he seemed to be getting over it, filling the void by engaging his itchy thumbs shovelling donuts. The cold blue tinge that had framed his lips by the time they got down from Dunnideer Hill was fading.

Fala really needed to talk to him about this sugar addiction—she cut the thought dead, not wanting to think about the future, not wanting to contemplate a time after the coming night.

Bartek had carefully placed his cappuccino in the cup holder on the dash, where it remained, untouched, causing a smudge of condensation to steam up the window directly above it.

Back in the warmth of the car, Fala could feel her consciousness fracturing like cracking ice. She felt frayed, like an old rope exposed to too much salt and spray on the main mast of a sailing ship. Soon all the fibres that held her together would separate and snap apart.

It was only a matter of time.

The pull to the sea was intensifying and her limbs grew heavier as her body fought to return to its natural form, creating an exhausting pain that threatened to overwhelm every other part of her. Concentrating was becoming harder. Her mind was suddenly enveloped in wet wool and the electric incisiveness of her thoughts was dampening down to nothing. She was acutely aware that she was at her most achingly vulnerable.

Undeterred, she forced her higher brain functions to carry on. She had too much to think about to succumb to the call of nature just yet. She was intrigued, trying to find a reason why she was behaving differently towards Bartek and why he, in turn, was not reacting in the way she had expected. He was not like any other watcher she had known.

Part of her worried that she felt like this every time at this stage in the cycle, that her connection to her current watcher was so strong she could not contemplate losing him. And yet, when she did, she would survive and compensate. But she could not recall feeling this anxious, this unsure in previous cycles. Normally she was focused on the upcoming ordeal, the coupling, the potential in it all. Why was this time so different?

It had to be because of Bartek.
What was the universe trying to tell her?

Sitting in the car, the sweet morsels of the bun exploding satisfyingly on her taste buds, she found herself re-commencing her replay of the memories of the times she had shared with him.

And what struck her most was how happy he had made her.

They had crossed the world, drinking in different cultures, meeting people, seeing wonders, searching for other fisherfolk and running from G'llaha and his cronies. Even so, the overwhelming feeling those memories engendered was one of joy. She had not spoken falsely on top of Dunnideer when she told him he had made her feel young again.

Unbidden, her memories came fast and uncontrolled, as if to emphasise the point . . .

In London, a city she had frequented so many times down the years, they had both ignored the cool November rain and taken long walks down along the embankment, past the London Eye, blinking on the other side of the dark river, and up to Tower Bridge. The tourist boats were tied up at the edge of the dark waters, all slumbering silently as they bobbed on the rhythmic, gentle waves.

The throbbing beat of the only party boat courageous enough to brave the elements drifted towards them and somewhere the blaring of a police siren ripped the air but all of it was a long way away. It had been late and empty and creepy. The ghosts of the past, with their guilt and secrets, were close, lingering on the cold drops of drizzle that blurred the city lights as they shimmered around them but huddling close the mermaid and her watcher had ignored the threat, safe in their impenetrable bubble of simple togetherness.

Fala remembered she had sworn like a trooper as her legs began to ache and the black water had insidiously called to

her, promising a release from her pain. She had ignored the
need, focused on Bartek instead and pretended they were
just a normal couple like the others they had seen walking
arm in arm.

They got a *Boris bike* from the rack to finish the journey.
She sat on the seat and Bartek stood on the pedals, a flash-
back to carefree teenage years neither could recall. When
they reached the stone steps of the bridge, he lifted her, light
as a doll, and carried her up to the roadway where they
hailed a cab, giggling and giddy, touched by something far
more intense than the rain.

London always thrilled her at first when she visited. The
culture, the sense of place, of history. A city that had stood
for more than a thousand years, eked out from the grime of
the Thames into something lasting and impressive. But
G'llaha's power was strong there. His constant manipulation
of its rulers to meddle in the affairs of other countries where
they should not had resulted in the violence and mayhem he
adored.

This brave city had suffered more than its fair share of
terrorist strikes down the years, all somebody's heroes, sacri-
ficing themselves with the name of a foreign god screamed
from their dying lips. Its inhabitants died, too, splattered
bleakly across the pavements. Flowers, lighted candles, and
latterly hashtags could not silence the keen mourning of
their wasteful loss.

And slowly Fala had come to see that G'llaha ruled this
place completely. Too many murders, too many ghosts,
haunted the historic city's dank and dreary underbelly, too
many lost souls wandered its streets after dark, and the mud
of the Thames began to subsume her, pulling her down into
a deep depression.

Memories of her loss snapped as hard as the winter wind.
But for Bartek's unfailing support and irrepressible encour-

agement, November in London, with its cold and clammy fog, would have been a shroud beneath which all her hope died.

Bartek, sensing her growing disquiet, had made arrangements. They moved on quickly.

The sun enlivened and re-energised her so they followed it. From his modest beginnings, Bartek had become a strong swimmer who enjoyed the water almost as much as she did. She showed him many wonders below the surface of the great oceans.

They travelled to Bali and watched beautiful sunsets over the islands as the volcanoes blew languid smoke into the haze. and in Thailand, where they approached Phi Phi Island by boat, as it rose from the sea like a fortress. Sheer cliffs towered overhead, giving way to beach-fronted jungle.

They lingered, delighting in the peace and freedom from the hustle-and-bustle. With no reason to be in a hurry, they visited the temples at their leisure and enjoyed a lady-boy show in Phuket. Fala pretended to be shocked by a particularly intricate scene depicting mermaids falling in love with humans and giving up their tails but could hold her frown for only a few moments before she joined Bartek's laughter.

They travelled around the Mediterranean, retracing their steps from the days just after they had first met and then further east to the historic sites of Italy and Greece. They did likewise around the Baltic, the place in the world Fala was most likely to call home. She felt the past like a cold shiver running along her spine as the places reminded her of her people, long lost.

In Perth, Australia, they swam out beyond the shark nets as Fala searched in vain for news of Yaringa, the last mermaid she had heard from in Oceania. A passing great white shark, more than five metres long, had stopped to exchange news with her and cast an interested eye towards Bartek.

Fala had made her watcher leave almost immediately—you could never trust a shark even when they gave you their solemn promise. In Fala's experience the need of their stomachs was always more dominant than their questionable morals. She hadn't liked the way this particular impressive specimen had scrutinised Bartek hungrily as he boasted about his liking for human blood after snaffling a tasty surfer a few weeks before.

In Perth, Scotland, they had lingered away from the sun and the sea in an effort to throw a particularly persistent bruiser off their trail. They had ended up in a frozen and smelly bed and breakfast too far from the ocean with only the River Tay to quench her water need.

But Bartek had made her comfortable, seeing to her every need. Hope was the flame that fuelled him. Through all of it, good times and bad, he stubbornly held on to the fundamental belief that good would triumph, that life was worth the pain it brought and it was there to be lived.

All would be well.

But there were bad times, too.

He never lacked in courage. On numerous occasions, not just on that awful night in Melbourne, he had taken a beating and dished out many in return to keep her safe. Thankfully he seemed to heal remarkably quickly for a human.

She remembered a hot, sticky night in Coco Beach, Florida, air thick as treacle, the thunder rolling around them and lightning sparking across the sky. With a touch of help from her shape sliding trick, Bartek had forced her out of the tiny bathroom window from which she had fled to safety and turned back to face the bruisers who were hammering down the door.

Battered and in pain, but ludicrously proud of his triumph, he had found her hiding under the pier the next morning and they had made their escape under cover of a terrific storm.

It had happened more than a dozen times and he never complained, never flinched, simply did what had needed to be done. He was stubborn and obstinate but never inelegant. Cool as ice, he had developed an indurate casing that made it easy for her to pretend he was invincible.

That conviction had been shaken only once. That was during their time on the Ille d'Orleans across the mighty St Lawrence River from Quebec. She remembered her panic, her feeling of complete powerlessness as she watched Bartek suffer.

Her watchers never got sick, or at least only a passing bug or sniffle that was easily overcome, but in Canada Bartek was very ill.

It started one evening as they stood at the kitchen sink doing something as mundane as the washing up. Without warning he had suddenly stiffened, let out a surprised snort and grabbed hold of the worktop to stop himself from falling as the contents of his stomach spewed forth with the velocity of a projectile.

At first amused by his incapacity, but then growing concerned, she helped him to bed. The vomit kept coming in a long, fluorescent, foul-smelling stream until his stomach was empty and then putrid digestive acids continued the performance, spewing upwards in a sticky yellow substance that smelt like bad beer.

Bravely, he had said it would pass, that he had suffered similar attacks as a young boy and after undergoing rigorous tests the doctors had pronounced them stomach migraines and that he would grow out of them, and he had, until now. He assured her it was a twenty-four-hour thing and he would be right as rain soon enough.

But it didn't get any better.

The vomiting ceased but only because there was nothing

left to bring up. The dull, dry retching continued and it was accompanied by a sky-high temperature, shivering and a growing, debilitating weakness. In his lucid moments, he begged her not to get a doctor, that it would pass but her panic grew as he was increasingly lost to the delirium.

In the end, she called out a local doctor, using psychic suggestion to persuade him to make a house call. The doctor didn't look in a much better state than Bartek, his hands shaking nervously and a hacking cough wracking through him but he examined the patient, rolled his eyes, staunched the sweat that sprung in sparkled beads on his forehead and said he would have to admit him to a hospital over the water in Quebec for tests.

After he had gone, Bartek refused point-blank to go and be poked and prodded by any medical person. It appeared the tests he had had to suffer as a boy to diagnose his stomach migraine had left him with a morbid fear of any repeat performance.

Fala despaired as his suffering shuddered and sweated hopelessly into its second week. She was cast in the new unfamiliar role of caregiver and was increasingly out of her depth. Washing him, cleaning up, trying to feed him weak, thinned soup that would stay down no longer than a matter of minutes was exhausting for her.

She tried her best but she knew it wasn't good enough and growing at the back of her mind like a silent malignant cancer, was the very real fear that she might lose him too soon.

They had planned to go south before the Canadian winter had begun to really take hold but the first snows came and soon the country slumbered beneath a chilly blanket. Great chunks of ice flowed down the St Lawrence and ice breaker boats chugged endlessly in an effort to stop the whole river freezing over.

Fala vividly remembered the paralysing fear, the inability to do anything to help. In anguish, she decided she would take him to hospital the following morning if he hadn't improved. He was sleeping, pale and plummeting, almost comatose. He had stopped talking completely and his groans, like a dying animal, were fading to nothing.

In that moment of extreme despair, she had done what she always did, done what the long years of her life had taught her to do—she disengaged, refused to acknowledge the fear. Shut it down, tight. *Fear couldn't hurt you if you refused to feel it, right?*

Bullshit.

It could insidiously creep into the marrow of your bones, numb every synapse in your mind, and ultimately strain every nerve in your body. It could silently and progressively take you over so that it defined you. You ceased to be yourself. You became simply a stagnant bag of bones and shit, inert, good for nothing. And that was Fala's greatest terror.

It all suddenly became too much.

She had left the cottage they were renting right on the banks of the river with the magnificent views of Quebec City, its lights twinkling in the frosty night, across the cold waters.

She could do no more and her own need for the water was so strong.

Plunging into the dark depths, she banished all thoughts of him, and instead embraced the sheer exhilaration the water always brought.

What would be, would be.

Calmness was a wonderful thing and within seconds of the water taking her, she was able to re-evaluate and plan. Along with the relief, the water brought back the memory of a similar time when the wasting sickness, with symptoms very much like those Bartek suffered, had plagued her folk and their followers. She had been very young and had not suffered but many, including her best friend, Uznam, had hovered on the verge of death, unable to swim, skin pale and grey, hovering on the edge of consciousness and moaning softly.

She remembered the frantic air of doom that hung over their city, the faces of her elders cracked and grief-stricken as they had tried to treat the afflicted with every possible cure but nothing had worked.

In utter despair, they had sent out dolphin messengers around the globe to all the other colonies. It had been Zuni that had responded, sending word of a potion made from the oarweed that grew in the kelp fields of the North Atlantic. The effect on the sick when they drunk the concoction was nothing short of miraculous and almost instantaneous, with all making a full recovery in a matter of hours after they drank it. Uznam had soon been jumping for joy and tearing around the city at full speed with her.

All those years later, as the revelation hit her, Fala had stopped swimming, letting the currents of the St Lawrence carry her as the memory warmed her, thawed her fear. A triumphant chord of sheer delight rang through her very soul as a bud of hope flowered gloriously. The quickening of something beautiful, so vibrant, so strong, it completely drowned out her fears. She had come up with an action, something she could actually do.

Of course, it may not work for humans like it did for her folk but at least she could try.

She called to a small beluga whale, one of the pod that had been caught in these waters before the last ice age and relished the area so much they had decided to stay when the ice had retreated, that had been lingering close by as if too shy to approach. He willingly showed her to a place where the brown oarweed algae was prevalent. She picked a handful and made her way back to shore with a sense of purpose she had not felt previously.

Trying valiantly to remember how she had watched her father prepare the draught all the years before, she worked with nervous hands and then rushed up the stairs with her prize, not even bothering to cover her nakedness.

Bartek was languid and drifting, lifeless like a deserted yacht on a becalmed ocean. Frantically she woke him, forced him to swallow the brownish muddy liquid she had made. He coughed and spluttered weakly and then fell back into the bed which seemed to have grown larger as he had shrunk into it, the illness stealing his strength and weakening him.

For a minute she thought nothing was happening and then, just as she recalled had occurred with Uznam, his whole body shuddered and he opened eyes that were suddenly focused and clear, the colour seeped back into his face below the ridge of razor-sharp cheekbones and his dimples flashed a weak, confused smile.

He was back with her.

"What the hell?" he breathed, more of a groan than a sentence.

She had grinned as unprecedented joy and relief washed through her. "I saved you," she responded immodestly as, under her breath, she thanked the universe that good old mundane oarweed worked on humans as well as on her own folk.

After that, it had been a glorious winter. She had swum for hours in the wonderfully bracing St Lawrence, playing with the belugas, dodging the ice and the ice breakers.

Recovering, Bartek sat on the rocks in front of their cottage, swathed in blankets, his breath misting in the freezing air, watching and laughing at their antics until it was warm enough and he well enough to join in.

Fala remembered it with a sweet, warm feeling fuzzing in

the depth of her guts and the unthinkable thought hit her then, cutting short her memories with one brutal slash—was that when she had fallen in love with him?

Ridiculous!

She almost let out a disbelieving gasp.

Fallen in love?

Now, there was a weak, human concept if ever there was one. It had never occurred in her world where her folk had frolicked and coupled only when the cycle dictated they must, to secure the future survival of their species. Their passion had been for the planet, satisfaction came from creating, from nurturing and protecting the wildlife that shared it with them. They cared for each other, of course, but to be in love with another soul, to commit your life, to be loyal to one person forever, to forsake all others, was simply not done.

And yet, she had heard the gossiping whispers, known of fisherfolk who had broken the law and fallen in love with one of their watchers. Scandal had ensued with the apparently weak unfortunate being thoroughly chastised and then ostracised completely, sent away to live a lonely existence once their human died, as they must, crushed, broken and alone.

The irony was not lost on Fala, the last mermaid. Now, she understood the biting loneliness her wayward kin must have suffered and for what?

But it was obscene to think of falling in love with a human. It was against the laws of nature and so unbecoming. They were such a backward race, naive and hungry for power, easily enthralled by G'llaha.

They couldn't even breathe underwater.

She stopped then, realising that, apart from the breathing underwater bit, the flaws she levelled at humanity could equally be ascribed to her own folk. Indeed, G'llaha had used such weakness to enslave and then destroy her people.

He bewitched them by giving them a little knowledge of shape-shifting, allowing them to walk on the land, but in accepting his support they had fallen into the same trap that mankind now tottered on the edge of—and then he had slaughtered them mercilessly.

She still remembered the elders' hollow words. "He is our friend, what can possibly go wrong?" She now knew from bitter experience G'llaha was no one's friend except his own.

Her mind was wandering fearfully and with great effort she forced it back to concentrate on the subject at hand.

Bartek.

There was so much that was good in her latest watcher, so much to love. He had given her everything she had ever asked. He existed in his own space and time, doing what she wanted with the graceful and competent poise of a dancer, untouched by the momentum of other's lives.

He had loved her, never without care but with a profound depth and always regardless of what he had received in return. He was different from the other humans she knew, different even from her other watchers, she felt sure.

Alone, distinct, he stood apart, like a brooding panther with raw courage pulsing through his veins. Why was it so impossible for her to accept that she had fallen in love with him?

Still, her mind recoiled from the thought, spun away from the possibility, shocked and a little disgusted. Her memory seemed suddenly unreliable and she could not believe what it told her. She was reeling, unable to find her equilibrium, rocking from one conviction to another with no commitment to any.

Did this always happen at this stage of the cycle? She had a vague feeling of deja vu as if she was re-watching a film she had seen years ago and could only remember when the scenes were revealed to her one by one. She wondered if this was always the case. Did she degenerate into this state every time? Deep down, her gut feeling was that this time was terrifyingly different but she could not find the clarity of evidence to believe it as a truth.

Her thoughts churned around her head, a maelstrom, a whirlpool of indecision. Just what she did not need at this time.

And then it was too late to ponder any more. Bartek's voice, as brittle as icicles swaying in a warm breeze, broke through her confused, swirling thoughts.

"We are here."

CHAPTER TWELVE

The song came from deep inside, the very essence of her being. It hummed through every sinew, vibrated every fibre and strummed her heartstrings with its beautiful melody. Bursting forth with the harmony of heaven, the song of angels, it was everything she was. It swirled and swooped like a young gull wheeling on the strengthening wind, joyful and free and yet it was more, so much more.

It was a lament as sad as the dying of the day, a chilling cry for souls that were lost, never to be found and an anthem, crashing like a terrible tsunami hitting land, a call to action that stirred the soul and emboldened the limbs.

All who heard it were instantly entranced, a sense of well-being, of hope, spreading through them like desert flowers blooming after rain but it was no placid, complacent emotion. It invigorated strengthened muscles, hearts, lonely and true, beat a terrific tattoo and anticipation soared, lifted to a joyous place where anything was possible.

It was simply irresistible.

The song spread outwards from the rock where she sat. A powerful wave, it touched everything. Fala knew the sea creatures felt it as it flooded through the ocean and the life on land heard it, too, as it rode the strengthening wind. All were immediately entangled in the fronds of its soaring beauty. Unable or unwilling to free themselves, they all gravitated toward it knowingly, bewitched by a true siren's call.

Fala's body was elated to be back in its natural form, every cell comfortable, no longer striving to hold its incongruent human shape. Now a new change was taking place, her consciousness at once disintegrating and elevating. She was nothing but the song stretching out in a thousand streams of being, some rushing backwards to the past, others forwards and still more dwelling in the present.

She was in many places at once and yet could process every one. She was omnipresent, huge, the centre of everything and yet a fractured whole that was everywhere.

And the song carried on.

It was mid-afternoon and a part of her looked out across the water from the rocky promontory. The sea was radiant, a translucent green almost turning to a rosy, petal-soft pink, seemingly hollow, empty but in fact holding on to its treasures with the desperate clasp of a lover who knows this is the last embrace.

It was perfectly still, no waves breaking on the sandy beach below her, as it conserved its power, biding its time, waiting. And the sky, pretty pearl-white clouds lighting the darkness above, while at the horizon the blackest storm raged, ugly and unfathomable. She knew she had summoned it with her song and it had responded, the bleakest night coming screaming angrily across the water towards her. Something told her it was part of the cycle. It always came.

And the song continued.

Some part of her was aware of her two watchers as they waited, further back inland from the rocky outcrop where she sat. She could sense their fear, their nervous anticipation as it sweated off them in the cold air. She could hear their words clearly, although she knew they were only meant to be whispers on the wind.

"She's got a weird fishy tail," Vipers uttered in sheer bemused wonder as he made his way to sit beside the fire Bartek had made. "She's sitting on that rock, proper beautiful, dipping her amazing tail in the water, the sea's a funny colour and she's singing that bloody amazing song. It's doing my head in."

Agitated, he scratched at the handle of the cricket bat he had found discarded in the small bothie that perched on the edge of the sand dunes along the beach, where they had spent the previous night and where they had left the car. Bartek had raised an eyebrow when the kid had grabbed his makeshift weapon and made a few violent practice swings but said nothing. "She's like one of those bloody beautiful fish women my grandad used to tell me about who used to lure sailors. Back in the day."

Bartek, his eyes lost in the flames, poked the fire with a stick. "That's exactly what she is," he replied, distracted.

"Christ, we best be careful."

Bartek pulled himself back to the conversation with difficulty and grunted. "It's too late for that, Vipers, for me, and, I fear, for you, too. We've heard her song."

"What do you mean?"

"I mean we are already caught and there is no escape, not from this. It's time to just do the best we can."

There was a loud rustle from the undergrowth below the finger of trees that reached out along the headland towards the rocky plateau on which they sat, their backs to the sea.

Vipers started. "What the hell is that?" He raised his cricket bat, clearly panicked.

At the edge of the firelight, a pair of red eyes glinted dangerously and moved towards them.

And the song continued.

Another part of Fala saw what she now knew was revealed to her every time at this point in the cycle. She had spent the last thirteen years living under a misconception. The universe did not care. It was neutral, ambivalent. It did not care in the slightest for any of its creatures. It simply set them in motion and stepped back, a child with a clockwork toy, winding it up, letting it go and waiting to see, with morbid disinterest, what chaos ensued.

It was the earth that cared.

Gaia, the earth, was her ally, her rock, her wisdom.

Gaia had created them all. They were all her children, born of this world, and she was as proud and protective as any mother could be. Fala's own people had forgotten that irrefutable fact. Humans in their affiliation with G'llaha had lost the link, too, but every other living creature understood, knew their duties, knew where their loyalty lay. It was to their home, their planet, and they would help Fala in her struggle, would do anything to keep her free.

And the song continued.

Fala felt the terrific boom as another psychic creature entered the sea. It pulsated into her awareness, stark and bleak, cutting through everything like a butcher's knife through meat on the bloody block, bringing the revolting hot stench of rotting offal and arrogance, burning flesh and corrupted power, embers and ash.

The Shape Shifter had entered the water and was in the game.

And the song continued.

Fala returned her awareness to the shore. Completely oblivious to the developments elsewhere, Bartek and Vipers were staring amazed at what was happening in front of them. Around them in the firelight, a number of animals had gathered. The first had been a badger, creepy eyes and all, snuffling into view, heavy body on slow legs. It had been swiftly followed by a number of dogs, some feral cats, and a highland cow, with more creatures following. Vipers' hand had tightened around his cricket bat but it had soon become obvious that these creatures meant them no harm. They simply waited, silent, senses alert and focused on the trees at the outer edge of the circle, ready.

"What are they doing?" Vipers asked in astonishment as the blackest crow alighted on a log to his left, intelligent eyes flashing in the firelight. It screeched a greeting and then fell as silent as the rest.

Bartek snorted. "I think they're on our side."

Vipers lowered his weapon suspiciously. "How can you tell?"

"Well, they're not biting your legs off or pecking your eyes out."

Vipers screwed up his nose as he peered distrustfully into the gloom. "It's a cow, not a bloody tiger."

"I think it's a bull." Bartek smiled wryly. "Wait and see. They will fight for her."

"How do you know?"

Bartek shrugged. "I just do. And we'll need all the help we can get when the bruisers come."

"What are they like?"

"Pussycats." Bartek was purposefully dismissive.

Fala noted absently that one of the cats threw them both a disgusted look at that comment. Bartek continued regardless, "You just need to keep moving and if all is lost and you get the chance, just run."

"And leave you?" Vipers looked hurt. "I wouldn't do that."

"She's the important one, always remember that. We have to keep her safe, that's all that matters, ever. Come back for her."

"You really love her?"

Bartek stood up in a flourish, throwing the stick into the fire. "She found me in a chip shop in Cleethorpes. Showed me the world. What's not to love?" he replied wistfully, somewhat uncharacteristically revealing just a smidgen of his past.

"But why? I don't understand." Vipers pushed. "I want to help but—"

"You will." The animals suddenly stiffened. Bartek moved towards the black, foreboding trees. "Now hide. I think they hear something."

"But why . . ." Vipers voice trailed off as his fright took control.

And still the song continued.

His odious stench was getting nearer, polluting the sea water like a lethal oil slick. Fala fought down her distaste, the urge to gag, and the wave of hatred that flashed through her. Her time was running out, her song almost ended.

She prayed that Zuni would come but all she could feel was the weak trace of him she had felt before. Where was he? She could not sense her mate nearing but she could feel the other creatures gathering in the water to protect her, the Moray bottlenose dolphins, small playful sea otters, grey seals, harbour porpoises, a number of whales both minke and pilot plus a basking shark called Basil. They all gathered in the deep water, waiting for her call.

And further distant she sensed a whole pod of killer whales who had forsaken their mackerel feeding grounds and were spearing through the water towards her. Would it be enough? If G'llaha was already in the water it would need to be.

And the song continued.

Fala flashed back to the trees and saw the girl, muffled in monochrome, her pale loose clothing, colourless like the cold, not softening her slender spikiness. Her platinum straw hair leaked around the edges of her woolly hat as she entered the clearing. In one hand she carried a pitchfork and in the other a fire extinguisher which she put down carefully at her feet.

"Who the hell are you?" Vipers demanded, his voice wavering almost as much as his cricket bat, revealing he was very close to losing his cool completely.

The girl ignored him, looked straight at Bartek. "My family have lived in the farm on the cliff over there." She nodded to where a brave light could be seen shining like a beacon in the gathering gloom. "Every thirteen years, when we hear her song, we have come to pay the lady reverence and to do our duty." She looked passed him then to the rocks where Fala sat and drew in a deep breath. "Wow, she is as awesome as always. And her song . . ." She shook her head as words failed.

Bartek waited for her to continue while Vipers shuffled impatiently but agreed, "She is awful bonny."

"My brothers would have come, too, as they have done many times in the past but they have all flown beyond. I am the only one left." The girl let the sentence hang, licked her lips before continuing. "My name is Finn."

"Finn is a boy's name." Vipers scoffed.

She threw him a lethal stare. "Short for Fionnula," she growled, raising the pitchfork rather aggressively.

"What are you gonna do with that?" Vipers asked, trying for calm confidence but only getting as far as whining uncertainty.

Finn just snorted and gave his cricket bat a withering look.

Suddenly the sky above them seemed full of whirling wings and squawking beaks. A whole flock of seagulls landed on the stubby grass at the edge of the wood and ravens alighted in the trees which seemed to sigh in welcome recognition.

And the song continued.

Time was no longer linear to Fala. She saw it all. She was the witness, the narrator of her whole story. Memories, fluid-like waves on the ocean, hit her in a never-ending ebb and flow. She saw her father and her family, her world, remembered the joy she had felt frolicking with Uznam, the pure innocence and luxury of feeling that life was wonderful and would go on forever.

She saw her mother's face and recoiled away. That pain was still too deep, too raw a wound to contemplate.

She saw every single one of her watchers, their names carved irrevocably on her heart. She would not forget them, what they had suffered to bring her to this place. She saw everything, all that she had lost and yet still she hoped. She knew Gaia was sending her strength, strength to endure, to do what must be done.

And the song continued.

Fala's consciousness hovered on many planes. Her mind was so big it seemed to contemplate many different instances all at once. Part of her fondly remembered her Bartek carrying her to this place where she now sat and, with the gentleness of a lover, tenderly placing her on the rock outcrop.

He had lingered before her, his boots soaked by the freezing sea water, wet briny droplets shining in the black hair that peered out from under his beanie, but he remained somehow untouched, safe within the confidence of his own agency, the air of danger and the explosive, seductive scent of him chasing the marine salt from her nostrils.

And, she had known deep in the depths of her soul, a braver man she had never met.

She had reached out and ran her hand along the ridge of his cheek. He moved his head slightly into her touch, his eyes, never leaving hers, a thousand fathoms deep, filled with words he wanted to say but never would. The intimacy of the moment was utterly unbearable and yet exquisitely satisfying. Neither could find the strength to break it. And so, they lingered, simply indulging in each other's company for one last time.

"I am sorry, Bartek," she began finally. "I never should have . . ."

He stopped her with a curt shake of his head, the rise of his hand and a stoic, "No."

She nodded, seeing all, for once understanding him at the very deepest level, knowing, that in his world, going further, apologising, would depreciate everything that had gone before, all that he had suffered to get them to this place and all that he faced this night. And that she would never do, for she knew she was his world and she understood that in all the very best ways, he was hers, too precious to tarnish with any unnecessary, worthless confessions.

Still, there was something she felt an overwhelming urge to say, something she should give him if this really was the last time they were together.

"Bartek, I—" But her voice, aching and anguished, got lost somewhere on the desperate road between her vocal chords and her mouth, and the precious words would not come. Try as she might, she could not say them, could not accept it, could not disclose it even now, even to him.

There were tears in his eyes and his voice faltered a touch but he smiled bravely, as ever accepting the meagre crumbs she gave him, and said, "Dear Fala, you are the reason I am. I would not change a moment of it." Then he bent forward to place a chaste kiss on her forehead. "All will be well."

He stepped away.

And still her voice was absent. She reached out and grabbed at the sleeve of his coat, stopping him. He stiffened and their eyes met once more.

"I know all of your names, right from the very first watcher to you, the last one," she had whispered hoarsely as her voice returned barely, defending herself from his attack on top of Dunnideer the previous day. "I will never forget you," she said, as proud and profound as the northerly wind, even though she hated herself a little, for those were not the words she wished to say.

He had gulped and nodded, eyes moist and shining in the silver moonlight but said nothing more. Then he had left her, screwing his sorrow and regret into a tight ball and thrusting it deep down with his cold hands into his pockets. His shoulders sagged briefly and yet he defiantly pulled them straight as he walked. Despite it all, he stayed strong. She knew he would wish this burden on no one but if it had to be borne, and they both accepted it did, he would take it on himself because he trusted he possessed the vigour and the vitality to carry it.

She watched him closely, each painstaking detail of his brave swaggering walk, and found comfort in the familiarity, like pulling on an old jumper and feeling it fit in all the right places.

He did not look back.

She knew he could not.

One solitary brackish tear ran from her eye over the contours of her smooth skin, dripping from her chin, downwards, to be consumed into the vast, perfect water of the ocean. And the moment that it hit, the cycle was completed. Deep inside her, the first notes of her song began to resonate outwards.

She could not stop it.

The cycle was coming to an end.

The thirteen years since the last time were past. She could no longer control her thoughts. She surrendered to the compulsion, let her consciousness shatter into even sharper splinters rushing outwards to the world, and let nature take over.

The process had begun and was inexorable.

Now, she prepared to allow the undertow to take her, to

slip under and give up her own feelings, to concentrate on the only thing that mattered—her survival.

Now, above all others, he was her last thought and it was fitting. She read his mind intimately as he crouched beside the fire awaiting his destiny and heard the words that swirled there as if he were standing next to her saying them. *Letting go is hard but the tighter you clutch hold, the more inevitable that you will lose that which you cherish. So, I'm letting you go, Fala. Swim free, my beautiful one.*

His last farewell.

Now it was all done.

A new tear followed the same course as the previous one, rolling to the sea down the protective fishy scales newly forming on her face.

And, at the moment the lonely teardrop hit the water, the festering storm, riding on the night's darkest wings, smashed into the coast, with all of Gaia's anger unleashed. Wild waves, spray and a biting wind battered the shore, lightning flashed across the sky and thunder rolled. A saturating rain, with huge smattering drops, and snow and hail, began to fall.

The very earth seemed to quake.

Fala took a last deep breath and then allowed herself to smoothly slip from the rocks into the receptive waters that reached up to her as the ocean accepted her with the sheer delight of a prodigal returned.

Above the noise of the storm, the psychic boom rang out for all to feel.

Nothing else.

Her song had ended.

Chapter Thirteen

Safe below the churning waters, flanked by her aquatic bodyguards, part of Fala waited as the obnoxious presence advanced towards her. She knew all the good people on land had battened down their hatches and retreated into the relative safety of their homes where they cowered, all Christmas cheer forgotten, worrying about trees that could fall at any moment, about the aerial potential of garden trampolines and wheelie bins that they should have tied down and about the long-term stability of their roofs as the gale raged outside. Locals would say it was as bad a storm as any in the last thirteen years and some, who could still recall, would hark back to the monster storm of '78. But that was for later. First, they had to survive the tempest.

And Fala waited.

A dark, malevolent blot, it appeared at the edge of her vision, travelling at terrific speed and growing at an alarming rate. As it grew nearer it divided into a number of beings, unearthly black shark-like bruiser creatures, all muscle and teeth, and in their centre a magnificent glowing red being, a creature of flame in the depths of the ocean.

Fala wondered if she was seeing the Shape Shifter's natural form at last.

The mob stopped before her, only a couple of metres distant, riding the currents that sought to wash them away, malignant, imposing and impressive.

The inevitable descent into conflict was so close it was palpable.

"Well, well, well." The creature's voice rumbled like the heat from a furnace, hard and uncompromising, hissing steam in deep water. "He said you were as lovely as your mother. But as ever he lied. You are far more attractive than that barren, dry old husk."

The psychic signature was very similar but only at this range could Fala tell it was not the same. This was not G'llaha but another.

There were more of his kind on earth. When had that happened? Shocked, she pushed the horror of that revelation away for a later time, concentrating on what the newcomer had to say.

"I am T'sasa, hive mate of G'llaha and, as I'm sure you will come to see, a better shifter, wittier and oh, so much more intelligent. A much-improved model if I'm honest. But who wants to be honest?"

Fala eyed him contemptuously. "I have always found it the best policy," she spat back.

"Really?" The flame seemed to spark in curiosity. "In that case, I'll start again, this time with more candour, Slider Girl." An assured chuckle rolled outwards before he continued. "I've seen what he did, very nice piece of psychic engineering, though I admit it begrudgingly. He has got talent. But you, you are no Shape Shifter. Thus by definition, I am superior to you in every way. He taught you to slide from your natural form to a human and back, and only that. A party trick, nothing more. You have no fire, no spark. Water is all you are, made of tears, made to be subjugated, made to amuse me."

"He taught me nothing." Fala snorted dismissively. "And if you're trying to win me over with your charm, it's failing."

The flame-like creature flickered again, this time seemingly a touch less confidently. "Oh, I get it, just because you say you want honesty, doesn't mean you do. Duplicity.

G'llaha warned me of that but he can be as guilty of it as anyone."

"If I am so worthless to you, why are you here, busting your ass trying to catch me?"

"My ass? Why, for amusement, Slider Girl, nothing more, believe me."

"Deception works both ways," Fala sighed. "But I will be truthful about one thing, I thought G'llaha was the most odious being in the universe. Now I see he has competition."

"Insults? Is that how you fight back? I give you truths and you resort to abuse. How very childish, I—"

As he whined, Fala lifted her arm and dropped it with a flourish. Her army of marine animals led by Basil, the basking shark, swooped forward to attack the vicious shark-like bruisers.

Within moments the sea was red with blood.

As she watched the writhing bodies fight, part of Fala wondered where G'llaha could be. Her heart froze when she realised there was only one place—up on the rocky outcrop where Bartek and Vipers were waiting. She threw her attention towards the land, becoming instantly aware of what was happening there.

The storm was roaring all around them.

Flanked by a number of animals, Vipers and Finn were snuggled down in the trees, hidden, peering towards the fire where Bartek sat, seemingly untouched by the storm, still and lifeless as a statue, simply waiting.

Fala could read her young watcher's unguarded thoughts with ease but Finn was not so accessible and Fala understood why, what her secret was.

"He's a brave man," Vipers muttered as his stomach rumbled, part of him wondering if he still had the Snickers bar in his pocket from earlier.

"Destiny is hard. You find your courage when you need

it." Finn shrugged, unseen in the darkness but Vipers felt her shoulder lose contact with his own. He missed her touch if only for a second. "But this time feels different. Maybe . . ."

Vipers snorted. "You really expect me to believe that you have done this before? When you're obviously younger than me."

Even in the gloom, he felt the icy calmness of her stare, appraising him, and Fala could see that it seemed to Vipers that this slip of a girl was looking into his very soul. His sense of unease, of frustration, and fear growing, he felt quite sick, all thoughts of chocolate forgotten which for him was huge, as Finn answered, "I wish my big brother, Aodh, was here. He was always the patient one."

Vipers bit back the thought that her family had the most ridiculous names as Finn hesitated, looking for the right words. "You are very young it is true but surely even you have learnt thus far that things are not always as they seem. The lady must have taught you this if nothing else. How long have you been with her?"

"Err . . ." Vipers considered, not exactly lying, but maybe embellishing the truth just a little, but he had an eerie sense that this strange girl before him knew the answer to all of her questions before he spoke it, so he went for an exact and honest reply instead. "About thirty hours, actually," he shook his head. "It's been a hell of a day."

Finn chuckled. "In that case maybe you are as naive as you seem." She gently squeezed his shoulder and Vipers had to admit he liked her touch. "Stay with me, I'll look after you."

"What's he like?" Vipers fought down the flush of macho indignation that flashed through him, figuring instead, if he was seen as an ignoramus, he might as well live up to the part and get some information in the process, since that had been sadly lacking from either of his two other travelling companions.

"Who?"

"The bad guy."

That silvery chuckle once more, like the lilt of a pure mountain stream tinkling over ancient rocks. At least he was entertaining if nothing else.

"How do you know he's the bad guy? Maybe that's us," she teased.

Vipers hesitated. The thought had never crossed his mind. "Because, because . . ." This leaving the sentence hanging seemed to be contagious but he had to admit it was useful when words would not come.

They were silent for long moments as the wind howled, cold rain splattered and the trees bowed down, bending in reverence to the power of the storm. The very air seemed heavy, charged with electricity as the lightning flashed across the sky above them.

Finally, Finn said, "Do you think it's happening by accident?"

"What?"

"The raping of the planet. The enslavement of your people. The colonisation of your world by another species."

"Well, I—"

"You hadn't actually noticed, had you?"

"Well . . ."

"Don't worry, very few of you have. It's his plan and he's very good at it. He gives knowledge, he appears to be on your side, but he only shares what will ultimately benefit him."

"Like what?" A part of Vipers was screaming *conspiracy theorist, run.* But he was too far down the rabbit hole to turn back now.

"The internal combustion engine," Finn continued. "A godsend, gave your people the chance to travel, to take control and boy have you used it but what has it done, what benefit has it brought, really? Yes, you can drive down to the shops instead of using your legs but you get fat and useless, and look at the fossil fuel you use. G'llaha comes from a planet with an atmosphere rich in carbon dioxide. That's no coincidence."

"And here's me thinking it was the natural development of my ingenious species." Vipers' tone was more defensive than he had planned.

Finn snorted. "And don't get me started on the internet and your iPhone."

"What's wrong with my iPhone?" Vipers' voice turned even more churlish as he felt the sudden, strong renewed pang of loss.

"Hive mentality."

"Hive mentality? I don't get it."

"The Shape Shifters are coming. Wake up!"

As soon as she said it, the scream of the storm was silenced, the wind ceased abruptly, and trees were paralysed in various stages of stooping before it. Everything seemed to stop and the air around the fire was frighteningly still. It was as if, after travelling at a thousand miles an hour the world smashed into an immovable brick wall instantly halting its forward motion.

At that moment G'llaha stepped into the firelight.

An intense and compelling cerebral howl of pain flashed through the firmament and Fala was forced to turn her attention back to the underwater fight. The water was now murkier as it blended with warm blood to form a soupy, murky substance. However, drawing on all her enhanced psychic skills, Fala could see the worsening situation distinctly.

Her defenders were fighting the underwater bruisers with valiant but ultimately wasted vigour. A group of dolphins had managed to surround a bruiser and swam around it in circles, creating a bubble tunnel that disoriented the beast. Once it was vulnerable, grey seals dived on it, forcing it down to the sea bottom where a couple of sea otters wrapped it in powerful seaweed fronds until it was immobile, then set about biting it with their sharp teeth until with a spurt of flame it shuddered and then vanished, leaving a slick of oily shadow on the sea bed.

One minor success was not enough with such a high-maintenance strategy and the other beasts, even though the very water itself was against them, causing their speed and manoeuvrability to be somewhat diminished, were picking off their assailants with ease.

The scream of pain had come from Basil, the gentle giant, who on seeing the battle slipping away, and against his passive nature, had swum all of his massive hulk, cavernous mouth wide open, at T'sasa. The moment the shark clenched his teeth into the flame the fiery pain wracked through him. But the courageous Basil refused to be put off and hung on to the flame even as it burnt through him, flambéing him with its intense heat.

Fala sent a pulse of psychic energy to obliterate the bruiser that was aggressively ripping apart one of the dolphins in front of her but there was nothing she could do to help Basil, surrounded by the shape shifter's aurora as his scream slowly faded but his teeth remained locked on their prey even as T'sasa struggled to free himself.

"Slider Girl, give it up," he hissed, his voice strained but still dripping with arrogance. "I will win. Fire boils water!"

Fala ignored his gloating and glanced around at the swirling mayhem, her heart sinking as everywhere she looked, her fighters were suffering under the severe onslaught. She attacked another two of the shark-like bruisers and was gratified to see them explode into inky black stains in the water, and the pilot whales they had been fighting swam away, although one left a hazy trail of blood to further thicken the water in his wake.

It was fair to say that T'sasa did have a point.

Where was Zuni? He should be here by now. There had been a window of opportunity as her protectors battled and kept T'sasa busy but that was fast receding as the bruisers got the upper hand.

The tingle of expectation was in her bones. Now she was ripe and ready but he was not here. Soon she would have to retreat or risk the unthinkable—the Shape Shifters capturing her.

As the possibility of another failure and its lethal consequences crystallised into her mind, she suddenly became aware of more dark shapes torpedoing into the fray. At first her heart sank further but then she realised with relief and a growing sense of hope, that these were orcas, the greatest hunters in the whole of the ocean.

Like a pack of wolves, they came on, fast and furious, surrounding their prey and giving no hint of weakness. Protected by his pod mates, using his massive tail to push the water to create a spinning vortex, and never getting close enough to touch the flame, the biggest killer whale pushed the still struggling T'sasa towards the surface.

As he moved upwards the Shape Shifter finally managed to release Basil's deathly grip and the charred remains of the basking shark, along with a major piece of the flame still held in those unyielding teeth, fell to the sea bed where it fizzled away to nothing.

T'sasa let out a pain-filled whimper, and too late, realised that he was now in great danger with a pack of ferocious killers after him, eager to maintain their ruthless reputation.

Fala allowed her body to rise to the surface, too, and watched, awed, as the flame, obviously hurt and increasingly desperate, struggled to right itself in the mountainous seas seeking to snuff it out.

Following its prey upwards the orca turned, raised its mighty tail high into the air and crashed it down three times on top of T'sasa. The flame flickered like a candle in a strong breeze, and then, falling in on itself, it lost its shape, collapsing to become a ball. It dulled from red to brown to almost black until it was barely discernible in the raging sea.

Although it was difficult to tell over the surge of the storm, Fala detected a weak psychic snivel, nothing more and certainly no brash pronouncements of superiority. Two young bottlenose dolphins swam in, clicking to each other in excitement, and, juggling the dull ball between them, took it towards the shore.

Fala sent her thanks to the orca, who nodded in modest but assured salute and, ignoring the angry burn on his tail, dived back into the depths to help his pod mates in their strategy of ramming, harrying and biting to dispatch their remaining enemies.

Fala turned her consciousness back to the land.

"Bart Buchan."

G'llaha's voice was as sticky sweet as warm treacle and as arrogant as a young stag who had just won his first rutting fight. The Shape Shifter was in human form, tall and assuming, hair dark, greying at the temples, giving him the essence of discernment and sophistication, and face chiselled from glacial ice, brutally handsome without the slightest hint of warmth in any pore.

He reminded Fala of the quintessential frightening abusive father, revelling in his patriarchal power, cruel beyond words, who knew he had all the answers to every question that he may be asked and would withhold them anyway, just because he could.

Fala wondered why she had never seen him in natural

form like she had just seen T'sasa. Was it significant? Was it a weakness she could use?

He certainly appeared to be stronger than ever as he walked confidently into the open space on the rocky outcrop. Around them the storm still roared, indignant and seemingly more furious that, for some reason, it could not now penetrate the peace of the clearing. G'llaha had the presence to hold it at bay enraging the storm that its potency had been diluted.

A conceited smile etched across his features, the Shape Shifter ignored its screams and concentrated his scorn on the man in front of him, the only other figure in the firelight.

"Buchan," G'llaha repeated. "It's a clan name from these parts, did you know? Maybe it's fitting you've come back here to die."

"The name is Bartek," Bartek replied, standing loose but firm in the face of the severe provocation.

"Indeed!" G'llaha laughed. "I always think it shows a distinct lack of class when a man prefers to hide behind the skirts of his woman, or in your case, behind her fishy tail."

Bartek spread his arms wide. "I'm not hiding."

G'llaha stopped a little distance from the fire and cocking his head, regarded the human. "There is something quite fascinating about you, Bart Buchan." He rolled his eyes. "If I had the time I would perhaps be curious enough to investigate further. Something is not quite right with you. But not tonight. Tonight, my hot date is waiting."

"She doesn't want you."

"That is not a consideration. I want her, so it will come to pass. I have a planet to govern. I do not have time for any form of resistance. Step aside or suffer the consequences of my wrath."

"You know I cannot do that." Bartek's brave voice was sure and strong.

"You are a fool like all the others who have stood in your boots in times past. She does not love you. She cannot."

Bartek shook his head. "That is irrelevant."

As she watched, Fala felt her soul quicken at Bartek's courageous stance. She knew with a dull, damning certainty what was about to happen and yet she was too far away to stop it. She should flee. T'sasa was vanquished, at least for a while, Zuni was not coming and her elevated consciousness would soon fade back to normal, to begin the cycle all over again. But still she could not turn away, could not desert her Bartek. She had to bear witness. This time she had to know how it ended.

G'llaha laughed again. "I am the fire at the centre of the universe. I am the flame that ignited your pathetic sun. I am the heat of victory and all those who stand against me will burn. You, Bart Buchan, will burn!"

As he finished his words, he made a gesture towards the fire. It leapt in response, red hot flames sprang upwards and out. Bartek threw himself back from the finger of flame that darted towards him, rolling away into the darkness.

Although the grass and the trees were wet, the sparks, dancing through the air with glee like malevolent gremlins, took hold instantly, and soon the whole ground seemed to be burning.

To add to the chaos, the area was suddenly filled with surging dark shapes as G'llaha waved his bruisers on. They were matched by the waiting animals, leaping from their hiding places outside the circle of firelight, howling their resistance, sharp teeth eager to bury themselves in their enemies' skin, and the battle was joined.

Fala saw Vipers fearlessly throw himself, cricket bat ready, at the dark figure of the bruiser that tried to pass his post. Behind him Finn, fire extinguisher squirting wild water, did her best to douse the flames but it was a thankless task.

The feisty sparks with a will of their own, jumping across gaps and feeding on anything that got in their way, no longer obeyed the laws of earthly nature. They erupted into fatal flames at every opportunity, smiting both mighty trees and lichen patches with no discernment whatsoever.

The air was filled with the sounds of the fight, growling, yelping, ripping and swearing. Sweetwood smoke lingered foggily above them, held in check by some invisible hand as the furious storm still crashed outside. It drifted across the scene, swiftly followed by the harsher stench of burning flesh. As well as the squeals and howls of the valiant animals, Fala could hear the psychic screams of the trees, crying out their defiance as the fires destroyed them.

She shuddered and made the decision to move her body from the safety of the deep water back towards the shore.

"Finn!" Vipers' scream pulled her attention back. His panic was pure and penetrating as the flames raced between him and where Finn fought, cutting her off completely. Finn had discarded her empty extinguisher and after whirling and slashing her pitchfork about her with much success, was now locked in a hand to hand struggle with a hefty bruiser. The flames, frenzied and formidable in their apparent freedom, rushed towards them.

"Finn! No!" Despair flashed through Vipers but the heat of the flames singed his eyebrows and he could do nothing but watch helplessly as the unearthly fire engulfed the fighting pair.

As he watched, mouth slack with amazement, suddenly the flames grew less bright as a brilliant white swan rose from the ground, wings beating in beautiful flight as it gained height and left the fiery fight behind.

Vipers was paralysed, standing wide-eyed in awe. He shook his head as if to clear it. "What the hell?" he muttered and then as the fire turned towards him, sniffing back his sobs, he turned and fled.

On the other side, G'llaha ceased directing the flames and gazed appreciatively at the mayhem all around him. Fala knew he had harvested much energy from the fear and the aggression, the dead and the dying. And there were many bodies of both bruisers and animals in various stages of burning, scattered across the churned-up ground to feed his ferocious appetite.

The flames were dying down, the fight almost ended. The defenders of the earth had been all but routed, those that had survived were limping away and a number of bruisers remained, stumbling about, looking for instruction.

With a sigh of satisfaction, G'llaha began to walk towards the water. As he moved away and took his power with him, the storm rushed in behind him, reclaiming the land with rain, sticky and crimson as blood, wetting the hot earth and dousing the evil flames into puffs of pitiful grey smoke.

G'llaha strutted as if unable to resist the chance to show off, changing shape at will through a range of different humans, animals and fantastical beings until he stood on the cliff edge, regarding the dark sea. To either side of him the storm raged, throwing itself passionately at the shore but before him all remained calm.

Fala felt the flux in the atmosphere, knew that Gaia was preparing all of her strength to allow her mermaid to escape. The mother would not allow her favoured child to be taken, Fala was too precious. A rush of selfish gratitude washed through Fala. She was not alone and she was certainly not beaten yet. Gaia still had many options to rely on. The sea was thicker, molecules banded tighter as if in desperate defence to stop the Shape Shifter entering. Fala sensed that, instead of moving towards the threat, she should be swimming away.

But still she could not.

Her consciousness hovered and, as she watched, a dark shadow, moving with familiar mesmeric grace, appeared from the area of the battleground that was still in flames, running fast and low.

"No," Fala whispered.

She could do nothing but watch as Bartek rugby tackled G'llaha from behind just at the moment that Gaia flung a massive wave to wash over the rock where they stood. They disappeared from view in the churning, writhing turmoil and when the wave drew back into the ocean, the rock was empty.

"No!" Fala screamed.

CHAPTER FOURTEEN

Fala lurched back into her own body with a painful thud. It took her only seconds to re-orient herself. She was swimming away fast from the underwater battlefield, leaving the orcas to hunt down the last of the bruisers. The water parted in front of her, easing her way, gently pushing her onwards. She squinted, looking ahead desperately, trying to pick out what was happening. In front of her was still murky but she could see the column of bubbles surrounding two, what appeared to be, struggling forms in the distance stretching up to the surface. She swam towards the disturbance.

As she approached she could clearly see the two figures thrashing and writhing wildly, silhouetted by fire as G'llaha's body spluttered uncontrollably from flame to human form and back again. She saw the glint of Bartek's narwhal knife being thrust downwards and the flame appeared to go out for a second but then reformed less bright than before.

She was almost there when the two beings parted. The sputtering flame, weak and intermittent, pushing upwards toward the surface, while the darker figure ceased flailing, dropped the knife and followed its descent as both fell deeper into the blackness.

It was a decisive moment Fala knew instantly—her enemy for so long was within her grasp. Maybe she could end this all this now. Stop the alien invasion of her planet. But there was no choice to make. Ignoring the obvious vulnerability of

G'llaha in his retreat, Fala dived for Bartek's sinking, motionless form.

They went down deep into the cold but her aquatic senses enabled her to take it all in, revealing his condition to her in every pitiful detail as she neared. His eyes were closed, a few bubbles drifted lazily from his mouth. His clothes were ripped and burnt, hanging from his frame and lazily trying to float upwards and away. In places the material melded with the raw red burns across his body where he had touched G'llaha's flame.

She reached out with despairing hands and the moment she felt him, the aura around them seemed to pulsate magically. The whole world seemed to hold its breath, caught at the second when potential fulfilment is achingly fingertip-close but still in danger of slipping away. She felt the intensity, the difference from every other time she had touched him in the past.

It was the mystical, magical power of this night.

Gaia's power.

The once every thirteen-year possibility brought to life.

In this place, at this time, it was true. Anything was possible.

She felt her soul shriek in surprise at the restoration to her of that most captivating of emotions — hope. Every single sinew in her being fizzed in delight as she was overwhelmed by a sense of Zuni's presence. She felt his blood zipping in Bartek's veins and it brought her real joy. The whole experience threatened to engulf her, carry her away on a wave of senseless expectation but she fought it, regaining her composure with difficulty to focus on the most important thing.

Weak and unconscious, Bartek was drowning.

She took hold of his head, pressed her mouth on to his and, using her gills for them both, forced life-giving air into his waterlogged lungs. He was limp in her arms, floppy and boneless, in desperate need of her aid but she was overcome as the selfish compulsion battled back, this time far too strong to resist. Everything fell away, the swirling waters, the panic, even Bartek's predicament. It was a moment of pure, perfect disclosure, like the second when a plane breaks through the turbulent clouds to be dazzled by the brilliantly bright sun in the peaceful blue sky beyond.

Suddenly everything was revealed to her.

She knew it all.

Finally, Gaia found the ability to show her most special child what she had been trying to tell her for years.

Fala saw Zuni, shattered and ruined after his last fight with G'llaha all those years before. She felt the misery and despondency of his failure. He knew he was dying, the wounds he had suffered were incurable, killing him inch by inch, a slowly releasing poison into his bloodstream that he could not combat.

She saw the bargain that the proud merman made. His solemn pact with Gaia to break the most sacrosanct law of nature, the one that no other fisherfolk had ever dared to disobey, to sell his soul in one last desperate attempt to further his line and save his species.

She saw the liaison with the pretty human woman, his seed planted, the boy he gave her and the promise he extracted from her. She saw the name *Bartek*, that the young woman in her bitterness at having been deserted and her ignorance of the message it conveyed, shortened to the name of her favourite cartoon character.

And she saw that great merman, her last lover, who had survived so much, shamble away, beaten and broken, unable to hold human form, leave the land, sliding back into the sea to succumb to his watery grave.

It was all so clear.

Fala understood why she had felt Zuni's diluted presence

ever since she had met Bartek. Why the poor girl Evie, his failed watcher, had to die when he rejected her. Why the wasting sickness had afflicted him and why the oarweed had cured him. Why Vipers had appeared before his time and, most of all, why she herself had broken another of her people's inviolable commandments and fallen in love with him.

It was Bartek's destiny to be here at this moment, to impregnate her with the hope of her species, to give new life for her people—twins—a boy and a girl almost genetically complete fisherfolk, to continue the line and then, like so many creatures in the ocean, it was his destiny to die, to drown . . . Bartek had been so much more than her watcher.

He was her mate.

The revelation sent her spinning down from the dizzy cloudless heights, kicking her back once again into her body with a shudder, and the movement seemed to wake him from his stupor. He struggled at first, trying to pull away from her mouth, gurgling with dread, eyes wide and panicked, floundering, arms thrashing feebly, hair flowing upwards with the currents.

Resolutely she held him tightly and he began to calm as strength from her that she gave unconditionally, flowed back into his damaged body.

She hesitated as the achingly frightening future yawned in front of her, beckoning her on, daring her, threatening to engulf her.

But she could not resist this unique opportunity even though she feared it would lead to tragedy. He pulled her closer, those beautiful eyes that had first attracted her so long ago, open, throwing off the shadow of pain, suddenly alive, aroused and seeming to accept the unfathomable impossibility of his predicament.

His arms, re-energised, enveloped her in a hug that was

long and heartfelt, and she felt the excited, electric emotion thrumming through him, buzzing with expectation, building the wattage to dangerous levels.

The invigorating water gurgling around them seemed to be gently caressing, supportive, urging them even closer. His tongue came to life in her mouth, whirling around her gums as he hungrily sucked in their air. Fala arched her back and shivered at the sensation. Her hands worked into his wild, flowing hair, pulling him closer, then slid down from his head and squeezed across his buttocks, beginning a hesitant search for the waist of his charred trousers, pulling them apart and then diving inside.

The pulsing shaft that greeted her was hard and hot against the cold water and the touch of her fingers wrung a bubbly grunt from Bartek as he pushed into her grasp. Fala felt her own arousal and she ground her pelvis against his thigh. Their mouths still locked and their bodies moved closer together. Fala took one of her hands and reached up to crawl it across his back, tickling along his spine and down his ribs again. The other teased across his balls.

Using his throbbing manhood to probe deep within the secrets of her fishtail, Bartek found her hidden delights and in his own rhythm, he plunged into her with long, even strokes. The sensations whirring through her were over-whelming, the feel of his flesh, the rhythmic pulse of his thrusts and his strong arms around her pushing her on-wards and upwards. In unrestrained eagerness, she let her nails trace more tenaciously, scratching across his back and down along his ass.

She could not see, could not think, could not do anything except receive him completely as he shoved his cock into her as far and as hard and as fast as he could.

Fala was swamped in sheer bliss.

The feel of his thick shaft moving in and out of her was

beyond anything she had ever experienced before, even her couplings with Zuni could not match this.

Past, present, future—everything else was forgotten.

There was only this moment. She wanted him inside her, as deep as he could go, and she lifted her hips, tail flapping, pulling him in even closer.

Bartek, seemingly obligated by an instinctive force he did not comprehend, could do nothing but push on. Fala felt his rhythm change as his climax neared and she wrapped herself tighter around him, matching him, their hips banging together recklessly in a coupling ten long years in the making. Each of his strokes rubbed against her most intimate place and she felt the tension peaking, splitting her in two with perfect dichotomy—never wanting this feeling to end and praying for the furious orgasm that was building inside her, an ocean wave nearing the shore, to break with violent rapture.

On a bed of beaded bubbles, the two of them pressed their bodies tight, shuddering and whimpering finally joined together, as ultimately, the crescendo was reached, the crashing wave hit, exploding within her, his seed shooting out of him, flooding her womb at the instant her own muscles convulsed. Overcome, she pulled her mouth away from his to let out a long, inarticulate growl, instantly lost as it rose up through the water. She felt the miraculous light within her, two separate pulsating drops of precious life burrowing into the safety of her womb and she pushed away, throwing back her head in a moment of intense pleasure, floating upward in her triumph.

Discarded, Bartek fell away. Entirely used up, with no energy to save himself, he sank down into the gloomy depths.

Coming back to her senses after the initial rush of ecstasy, Fala looked around for her mate. She finally spied him lying motionless, spent, wasted, utterly destroyed, curled into the fetal position, body broken, his skin shining white, pale almost translucent, a fallen angel on the dark bed at the bottom of the ocean.

Fear rushed through her, chasing away the elegant bliss of the past minutes, the soft afterglow that bathed her brutally shattered as sheer fright ripped through her.

The water, once welcoming and pushing them together had transformed. Now the currents forced her away, pulling her to the east, to the Baltic, where safety lay.

She fought against the compulsion, slashing her tail strongly to maintain her position and then to move forward, going down until she had him in her arms again. She felt the spark, the spirit of him inherited from his father, distant and fading but still there. Again, swimming upwards, she clasped her mouth around his and forced air into him. Brackish water filled her own mouth from his when she sucked but she spat it out and continued.

Finally, she broke the surface, shifted to her own lungs, and, ignoring the water pulling her away, set out bravely for the shore, Bartek's lifeless body draped across her arms, in the same pose he had carried her when she had needed to be rescued so many times in the past.

The night clouds above were still angry black but the storm was passed, the sea softening and the wind dropping. The furious tempest that had broken the backs of the puny supply ships waiting down the coast outside Aberdeen's safe harbour was now nothing more than a soft breeze lightly ruffling the feathers of the gulls swooping above.

Her mission accomplished, Fala's heightened consciousness was fading as the coming dawn lightened the horizon behind her. But she sent it out and quickly located Viper's shivering aura. Praying that their link had matured enough over the passing hours, she sent him an urgent instruction.

Of Fionnuala, daughter of Lir, she found no trace.

Her prayers were answered as she rode on to the beach on a wave like the most skilful surfer and saw Vipers, knee-deep in the freezing water waiting dejectedly, lips that pretty shade of blue to match his eyes and teeth chattering loud enough to wake any drowned sailor whose watery grave was in the vicinity.

She slid into her legs, wobbly feet landing on to the sand, she stumbled but pushed herself on towards him.

"What the hell happened?" Vipers shouted above the crash of the breakers.

She ignored his redundant question, instead forcing Bartek's body into the younger man's shuddering outstretched arms.

"Save him," she screamed.

"I don't know . . ."

She shook her head to silence him. "Save him," she shouted again seemingly to the air but really to the omnipresent Gaia who alone had the power to grant her wish. "He gave everything for you. Save him. Now!"

There was silence except for the cyclic *whoosh* of the breakers. Freezing spray coated them and the treacherous sand beneath Fala's feet seemed to shift. She glanced down at Bartek's beautiful, lifeless face, pale as porcelain, felt her heart break as her desperate understanding grew and she saw the price Gaia would make her pay to answer her demand. What it would ultimately cost her.

She staggered as the next wave sought to push her from her feet and she could hold her form no longer, her body betraying her in favour of the command from the earth that birthed her.

She was ripped away from him, falling backwards into the surf, legs gone, her tail splashing the foam as the undertow sucked her back in. In the chaos of the breaking of another wave, she heard Viper's triumphant shout. "He's opened his eyes. Fala—"

"Tell him," she spluttered, beached, ironically almost drowning as she fought the compulsion of the sea, fought to retain her waning human form. Those precious words still would not come. And she knew with stunning clarity, she would not say them now.

Not here.

Instead, her vision moist and blurry so she could no longer see, but the scene seared into her memory cells, she called. "Tell him I will return."

And then her heightened consciousness faded to nothing, a light winking out into darkness forever, the drops of life in her belly called to her to keep them safe, her gills returned and she allowed Gaia's strong current to re-float her, to pull her out, to take her where it wished.

The sea claimed her.

CHAPTER FIFTEEN

Vipers stood shivering in the water, bereft, heart sinking and panic rising as Fala's fishy tail disappeared under the waves and was gone. He glanced about wildly, looking for some assistance.

There was none.

The only solace he could clutch at was that morning would soon arrive. The night was on the run as a line of pinkish light swelled upwards from the horizon but the cloudless sky above remained the darkest black, imprinted with twinkling stars like diamonds on the water, a thin sliver of silvery moon shining weakly.

Over by the rocks, in the trees, he could see flashes of blue lights. Somebody must have seen the flames in the night and called the emergency services. And to the other side, he could see the orange lights of the little town blinking sleepily in the growing grey light.

Everyone was too far away.

He turned, straining with the dead weight in his arms and made his laboured way back to the beach. He was thoroughly miserable and more than a little scared. His jeans were sodden to above the knee, taking on that heavy, depressed air that wet denim does so well. The rest of him was not much drier. Cold water dripped from his hair and the end of his nose and the sorry squelching at every step from his completely ruined trainers was the only way he knew his feet were still attached to his body.

There was a day in the not too distant past when he

would have left everything and simply scarpered but not this time. This time a flower of responsibility seemed to have bloomed deep inside him and although he swore long and hard as he struggled, he struggled nevertheless.

Once away from the sea's freezing, fingering reach, he gently lay Bartek down on the drier sand.

"Shit, what do I do?" he muttered, regretting that he had, when he bothered to turn up, never paid attention in first aid classes at school, preferring to sit at the back and play on his phone on the few days he had attended. He vaguely remembered some shit about clearing the airways and checking for a pulse but wasn't confident he could do either.

However, as if to answer his question, Bartek let out a long, deep groan, rolled over on to his side and began to draw up massive hacking coughs that wracked the whole of his body. Black, freezing water spewed forth and Vipers only just managed to miss another soaking by staggering like a drunken old man out of the way. To Vipers the spewing seemed to go on for hours as he fell to his knees beside the shuddering form, feeling useless.

Finally, the coughs seemed to dissipate, and, moaning feebly, Bartek rolled over onto his back, shivering even more violently than Vipers was. They were both soaked to the skin with freezing water, pebble-dashed with sand and Vipers knew hyperthermia was a very real threat. The beach, drab and colourless in the dawn light, was still deserted. Sighing deeply, Vipers realised there was nothing for it but to struggle as best they could towards the flashing blue lights in the hope that there were paramedics there.

Bartek's eyes, bloodshot and raw, were open and he nodded weakly as Vipers made to lift him. He was periodically coughing and vomiting and had difficulty holding his head up as Vipers got him vertical. He lolled pathetically like a rag doll, resting his head on Vipers' shoulder but managed to put one foot in front of the other as they began to move.

They were about halfway across the beach, veering on a diagonal course towards the rocky outcrop when the peel of the bells, ringing out proud and defiant, from the village behind reached them.

"Screw it," Vipers muttered. "It's Christmas Day. Where the hell is Santa when you need him?"

Words were too much for Bartek, who was hovering on the lucid side of conscious with difficulty and could let out only a weak groan. But Vipers did get an unexpected and unwelcome answer.

"There's no imaginary benign being coming to rescue you, boy. The universe doesn't work that way." The voice boomed out from the dunes to their left as G'llaha strode into view.

"Shit." Vipers breathed as pure, vivid terror stole the strength from his legs, and he and Bartek fell forward into the clinging, dry sand.

"On your knees, is indeed fitting," G'llaha chuckled humourlessly as he moved towards them.

It was, however, a greatly transformed Shape Shifter that Vipers saw. He no longer gave off the air of being completely untouchable. His left side was slumped at a strange angle, and a gaping knife hole so wide you could see the dunes behind him through it could be seen distinctly around where his heart should have been.

Even his voice was not quite as magnificent but tainted by sharp groans of indignant pain. Vipers wished he had his cricket bat handy so he could have taken advantage of this obvious weakness and play a heartfelt shot that would send the bastard into oblivion. But he had mislaid his bat somewhere that he could not now find the energy to recall. Instead, although G'llaha was clearly injured, it was obvious to Vipers that both he and his companion were in a far worse state.

There would be only one winner in this scenario.

Vipers could feel Bartek shivering uncontrollably beside him and wished he could move to at least share body heat with a man he barely knew but somehow felt a stronger affinity to than any other person he had met in his life, but his fear held him rigid, a statue frozen to the spot.

He felt the Shape Shifter's hot gaze move from them to a ball of dimly glowing light which had appeared to Vipers' left.

"G'llaha!" The voice calling from it was similarly faint.

"What did you do, T'sasa?" G'llaha rumbled with vehemence.

"Nothing. Those fish. Ripped half my body away." The voice was weak but still outraged at such audacity as it continued. "My flame is fading. I need to rekindle."

"As ever you are such a disappointment to me," G'llaha bit back. "Still you lie! You screwed her. I sense it. Do you think me stupid? The world has changed, her aura is brighter. It positively glows. The fish bitch is impregnated!"

"I didn't get near her."

"Liar!"

"You are a fool, G'llaha." Marshalling all of his remaining strength, T'sasa fought back with words designed to wound, his light ball now flashing angrily. "You have dwelt on this cursed planet for too long. You have gone native. Look at you, you can hardly shift at all! Your power is failing, for all the sustenance you get here. The witch is eating away at you all the time with her bacteria, her viruses, and microbes. Our Queen will not be pleased."

The flame flashed from G'llaha's outstretched hand. There was a squeal of surprise like an indignant pig, the glowing ball flickered and then went out forever, leaving only a sticky, black shadow of wax on the white sand.

His competition brutally eliminated, with hideous purpose G'llaha turned his furious gaze back to where Vipers and Bartek still knelt.

As the horrific argument had played out, Vipers had considered crawling away. The rocks were not that far and if he could get there he could surely get the attention of the police up near the fire. But his limbs would not obey his command, would not move except to shiver violently and so he remained in place, miserable and motionless. Beside him, Bartek seemed to have stopped shuddering. Instead, he was strangely still, awaiting his fate with surprising and, to Vipers at least, admirable, stoic alacrity.

Apoplectic with rage, G'llaha yelled, "I will fry you both!" All previous composure had seemingly been chased away by the overpowering intensity of the hate that T'sasa had enflamed with his words.

He lifted his arm, and Vipers, heart thumping like a drum in his chest, was not brave enough to face his own death. Instead, he closed his eyes and shrank away.

The anticipated flesh-obliterating fire did not come. In its place, an ear-shattering screech cut through the air. Vipers opened his eyes and saw a massive swan. With proud neck arched and white wings flapping bravely, it hissed its rage and flew straight at the Shape Shifter.

The two creatures wrestled for a moment in a confusion of flame and feathers. The sick stench of burning flesh ripped through the air and then there was a terrific bang and the flame disappeared. The bird fell from its last doomed flight with all the grace of legend, almost too slowly to the floor.

A beautiful, dying swan.

It did not move further.

A strange silence settled over the deserted beach. It was as if the whole world paused for breath, needing time to process the horrifying events. And then the stillness was punctured by a lone seagull's lamenting cry of sheer grief, quickly followed by the crash of the waves behind.

"Shit!" Vipers breathed as he slowly amassed the energy to climb to his trembling feet. Stunned, he turned around on the spot, taking in the sepia scene around him.

Beside him, Bartek groaned and collapsed into a saturated, sand-covered heap, while in front of him the lifeless body of the majestic swan had somehow transformed to that of Finn. Her pale clothing was now tainted and smudged with blackened burns, but she lay as if sleeping, her features set in a sad smile framed by her flaxen hair spreading out like a fan on the sand beneath her.

Vipers gulped.

Shivering uncontrollably, he had never felt so alone.

Above him it appeared the Earth, in celebration of a triumph although at great cost, had thrown back the quilted dread of night and, but for a few light saucer-shaped clouds that still lingered, a clear, cool, cerulean sky was revealed.

In the east, however, the reflection of the sun brightened the horizon with a bloody, crimson dawn, a warning that the fiery threat still lived and victory in one battle did not constitute the end of the war.

The village bells, oblivious to the events of the night before, continued to bravely peal out through the gloom of the bay, heralding the foolish and misconceived hope that only Christmas can bring.

CHAPTER SIXTEEN

And the watcher watched.

He watched the rugged coastline and the sandy beaches, the rocks and the sand dunes, the river estuaries and the crashing waves, never missing a thing. He saw everything and immediately discounted it all, for it was never what he desired.

He sought the sight of a weird fishy tail.

One dark night, he had seen an opportunity to end it all and, courageously, regardless of his own fate, he had thrown himself at the chance. He had been burnt by the fire that sparked his solar system's sun, the furnace that burned from the beginning of the universe. The puckered, pale scars where the flame had charred his skin and gone far deeper, scorching his very soul, were testament to his agony.

And, instead of an ending, he had found a glorious, if short lived, beginning.

He had sucked solace from the ice at the centre of the poles, a relieving balm of gentle silence for his screeching wounds. And then, borne on the wings of the mightiest storm, he had rocketed higher than any mountain and plunged deeper than the most inscrutable subterranean trench. The earth showed him all of her magnificent wisdom and her nurturing power through the passionate touch of his lady, the fair water maiden of his dreams. His heart soared to unimaginable planes, higher than any mortal had any right to climb.

He fleetingly tasted the very best that love can be.

And she had promised him more.

She would return.

Addicted to his hazy, yet ecstatic memories, longing for her touch, he gazed with eyes that swirled with every colour of the ocean, out to sea and he watched.

A good man in an uncaring world.

Watched and waited.

Perhaps he's watching still . . .

EPILOGUE

Far, far away, another watched, too.

Pulled from her tedious indifference by the unexpected news she received. The unthinkable had happened. After centuries of fusing, years of interfering and soldiering, at the very point of another predictable victory . . .

. . . a planet had repelled her final advance, had killed her missionary soldiers, had thrown off her yoke and rebelled.

Her anger was voracious, matched only by her surprise that such resistance was even possible in this universe that she had welded into what she wanted. Many would pay for this failure. She let out a scream of fury and threw a fireball that enveloped and extinguished the flames of a number of her unfortunate sycophantic subjects who had taken the chance to bathe in her light and were altogether too close. She was not in the least bit distracted by their ashy demise. She was too entranced by the emotions that flashed through her.

Because there was a delicious attraction here.

A rebellion?

A sister who refused to succumb?

How utterly enticing this was.

Feeling a buzz of excitement crackle through her well-worn complacency, she searched for more data. Where was this place? Who was the sister who stood against her? What was her power?

Gaia.

Puzzled, she did not know the name, had never heard it and certainly did not recognise her as a threat.

She had no knowledge of why or how this apparently weak sister on the edges of a bleak and pitiful star system could possibly withstand her onslaught. She could find nothing that could account for this seeming ability to quench her fire.

Yet it appeared that she had done so.

This Gaia.

And the electrified itch within her grew into something more substantial and more terrifying. It was at once alluring and infuriating—the possibility that she had finally found an adversary able to break down the walls of smug boredom that her hitherto infinite catalogue of successes had built around her, was, in that moment, beguiling beyond belief.

But she was perceptive enough to realise that this wanting would soon turn to an annoying irritation that would burn into the very soul of her, that she would be unable to tolerate.

She could not lose to anyone at any time.

Her conclusion was simple.

She would enjoy the thrill of battle, so long since forgotten.

But she would not be denied.

Not by anyone and particularly not by a weak sister who had only one pathetic planet to call her own. She would make an example of her. She would destroy her and everything she had, and the universe would see the futility of standing before her power.

And so, with angry retribution and merciless rage, she turned her undivided attention to the unsuspecting planet . . .

. . . Earth.

YOU MAY ALSO ENJOY THE FOLLOWING FROM EXTASY BOOKS INC:

Aquatic Attraction
Charlie Richards

Excerpt

Carlye kept her forced smile on her face as the last of the prospective investors strode out of the conference room, leaving her alone with her boss. She'd just about died from embarrassment when she realized the man from the lobby was sitting in the room. She'd been unable to meet his eyes even once.

"Well done, Carlye," Vance said, grinning happily. "I'm going to make certain that all of our guests make it out okay."

"Thank you, Vance. If you need me for anything else, I'll be in my office." She watched him nod and leave the room. She turned to collect the rest of her paperwork and shut down the computer used for her presentation. A moment later, Carlye nearly leaped from her skin when she felt a hand gently caress her arm. Spinning around, she found the investor from the lobby a couple steps behind her.

He grinned, and the action sent her heart beating double time. Every cell in her body sizzled with awareness of his innate masculinity. "I apologize for startling you. I said your name, but you didn't seem to hear."

Carlye could believe that. Her thoughts could consume her to distraction. "It's okay, I was just thinking about the presentation. Is there something I can help you with?"

The man nodded and held out his hand. "I'm Niall Karson. You made some interesting points, and I'd like the opportunity to speak with you in more depth about them."

"Oh. I see." She berated herself for even hoping he could be here because he had an interest in her. Carlye reached up and took his hand. The zing of awareness almost dropped Carlye to her knees. Warm heat flooded up her arm and through the rest of her body. Holy crap! What was that?

"Have dinner with me." His words sounded more like a demand than a request.

Her brows shot up, and Carlye tried to disengage her hand from his. Niall refused to let her go.

"Have dinner with me this evening, please," he asked, softening his tone.

She heard the huskiness in his voice and realized she wasn't the only one affected by the handshake. "I'm sorry. I can't," she murmured. "It's against policy to date clients."

At that, Niall grinned. "I'm not a client yet," he murmured.

The heat flooding Carlye's body suddenly pooled below her stomach. Where did this attraction come from? She'd never been turned on just from a handshake and a smile. Besides, she didn't even know this man!

As if reading her thoughts, he tugged her hand, pulling her flush to his chest and wrapping his free arm around her waist. Niall splayed his large hand across the small of her back, holding her close. Carlye's skin seemed to tingle at every point where her body pressed against him. She felt too close and yet not close enough. Her free hand landed on his arm, and she bit back a moan when she felt the hard muscle hidden by his suit jacket. Niall's head lowered toward her face, his blue eyes glowing with intensity.

"We'd be doing so much more than dating, sweet vixen," he whispered, his lips an inch above her own. "I can sense your body's heat. My own mirrors it. Don't fight the attraction."

Then his lips covered hers in a slow, thorough kiss. He nipped her bottom lip, and Carlye gasped in surprise. She felt Niall slide his tongue into her mouth, stroking her tongue and causing the heat in her belly to rage into an inferno. As Carlye slid her hand over Niall's biceps, she realized it wasn't to push him away, but to clutch him closer. The fact gave her the strength to break the kiss.

Staring up into his blue eyes, Carlye saw that Niall's breathing was just as ragged as her own. "We can't do this," she whispered when she managed to get enough air into her lungs.

Niall's eyes narrowed slightly. "I'll pick you up at seven. Bring your charts if it makes you feel more comfortable. Do you have a food preference?"

Surprise shot through Carlye. The man refused to take no for an answer, and truth be told, she felt flattered by his persistence. So, instead of doing the sensible thing, she answered her body's call for his. "I'm not picky. Whatever you want is fine."

"Good." Finally, Niall's arms loosened. "I'll see you in a few hours." He gave her a quick, chaste kiss and strode from the room.

Carlye stood frozen, staring after him, for several minutes. She could still feel the heat of his body, the strength of his arms around her, and the warm, possessive press of his lips. Finally, she pulled herself together, gathered her files, and left the conference room. The nagging question of why he was so adamant about seeing her niggled in the back of her mind.

ABOUT THE AUTHOR

Jack Crux lives and works in beautiful Aberdeenshire in north-east Scotland, taking as inspiration the wonderful scenery there. Find out more by visiting the Jack Crux Facebook page or tweeting JackCruxofit@cruxy95

www.ingramcontent.com/pod-product-compliance
Lightning Source LLC
Chambersburg PA
CBHW060827120626
46557CB00001B/402